Praise for
Stella Díaz Has Something to Say

2019 Sid Fleischman Award winner

★"Fans of Clementine and Alvin Ho will be delighted to meet Stella."
—*School Library Journal*, starred review

"Readers should easily relate to Stella, her struggle to use her voice, and the way she feels caught between worlds at school and at home."
—*Publishers Weekly*

"An excellent, empowering addition to middle grade collections."
—*Booklist*

"A nice and timely depiction of an immigrant child experience."
—*Kirkus Reviews*

"Readers will agree with Stella's mother
and brother that she is, as her name suggests, a star."
—*The Bulletin of the Center for Children's Books*

"A rich narrative."
—*Horn Book*

Also by Angela Dominguez

Stella Díaz Has Something to Say

STELLA DÍAZ NEVER GIVES UP

¡Así es!

ANGELA DOMINGUEZ

SQUARE
FISH

Roaring Brook Press
New York

SQUARE FISH

An imprint of Macmillan Publishing Group, LLC
120 Broadway, New York, NY 10271
mackids.com

STELLA DÍAZ NEVER GIVES UP. Copyright © 2020 by Angela Dominguez.
All rights reserved. Printed in the United States of America
by Berryville Graphics, Martinsburg, West Virginia.

Square Fish and the Square Fish logo are trademarks of Macmillan and
are used by Roaring Brook Press under license from Macmillan.

Our books may be purchased in bulk for promotional, educational, or
business use. Please contact your local bookseller or the Macmillan
Corporate and Premium Sales Department at (800) 221-7945 ext. 5442
or by email at MacmillanSpecialMarkets@macmillan.com.

Library of Congress Control Number: 2019941021

ISBN 978-1-250-76271-9 (paperback)   ISBN 978-1-250-22912-0 (ebook)

Originally published in the United States by Roaring Brook Press
First Square Fish edition, 2021
Book designed by Elizabeth H. Clark
Square Fish logo designed by Filomena Tuosto

5 7 9 10 8 6

AR: 4.2

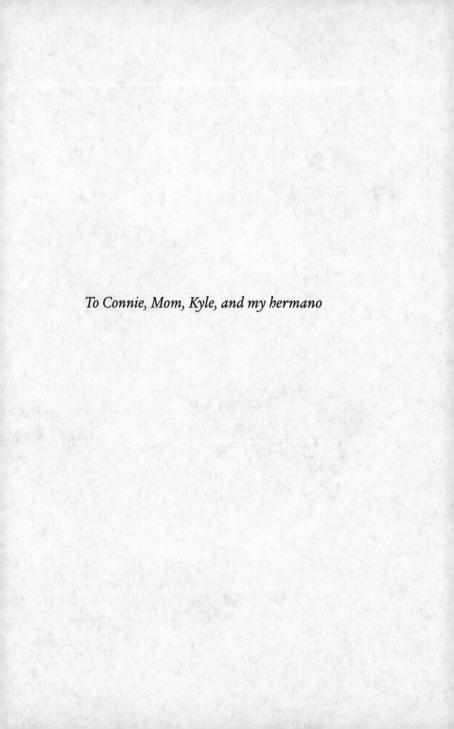

To Connie, Mom, Kyle, and my hermano

Chapter One

It's been eleven days, and summer is already a slow crawl. Everyone strolls around like they're floating on an inner tube on a lazy river. No school means there is nowhere I have to be. This can be awesome. Some days, I ride my bike for hours with my best friend, Jenny, or go swimming with my big brother, Nick. Unfortunately, on most days, the only place I am is stuck at home. I've got my work cut out for me. It's going to be hard not to be bored.

Today I begin by searching the house. I want to find my own mystery caper. It'll mean a new adventure for me. Then I'd have to spend the entire summer solving it! At least that's what happens in Nancy Drew.

I find a few fun things like *Journey to the Center of the Earth* in *español*. A book can be an adventure, but the Spanish is too hard for me to read.

"I'll read it when I'm older," I say to myself as I put the book aside.

In Mom's bedroom, I find a ring tucked away in the bottom drawer of her jewelry box. Maybe it's the ring from *Lord of the Rings*! Then I read the inscription inside. In cursive script it reads *"para mi güera."* *Güera* is Dad's nickname for Mom since she has light-brown hair. No mystery here. It's Mom's wedding ring that she no longer wears since the divorce.

I spy around Mom's closet next. Zero luck, but seeing Mom's "business attire" reminds me of how *ocupada* she is at work. All I know is if Mom were with me during the day, summer would be more fun and there would be more yummy *albóndi-gas*. Mom's meatballs are guaranteed to make any situation better.

The last place to explore is my big brother's room. As I approach his room, Nick stops me.

"Off-limits."

Then he walks toward the front entrance of the house.

"I'm heading to work, sis. Be nice to Linda. She'll be here in a minute."

Not exploring Nick's room doesn't bother me too much. I'd rather discover some secret compartments. Not boy stuff.

With my snooping at an end, I head back to my room. Time for another brainstorming session. Hopefully Jenny can help me brainstorm later when she's not at dance camp. Then again, if she were here with me now, I wouldn't need to think up fun things to do.

Then I look over at Pancho, my betta fish.

"I know what to do."

Time for plan B.

Chapter Two

Now plan B is not bad at all. It's actually great. The "B" in plan B might stand for the BEST idea.

My plan is to continue what I started in Ms. Bell's class and study as much marine life as possible. I'm hooked! Like Jacques Cousteau said, "The sea, once it casts its spell, holds one in its net of wonder forever." Scientists predict that we've only seen 5 percent of the ocean floor. It makes sense, since they are miles deep and cover 71 percent of the earth.

I'll need to know more about the oceans, too, if I'm able to go to the Shedd Aquarium summer camp.

Mom helped me apply a little while ago, but we haven't heard anything. I even included with my application a persuasive essay on how I wanted to be the next Jacques Cousteau. To top it off I attached pictures of my animal project from Ms. Bell's class.

I really hope that I'm accepted into the summer camp. This way I'll be doing something memorable this summer just like everyone else I know. Like Jenny has her dance camp. She is even going to have a big recital. One of the biggest in town, she says! Then Nick has his first big job. It's only part-time, but he gets a paycheck like an adult. Mom is so proud of him. She wanted to frame his first paycheck, but Nick said no. He wanted to keep the money more. I want to make Mom proud of me, too, but I can't get a job. I'm too young to work! All I know is if I don't have a project or adventure of my own, my summer will be Boring with a capital B. I'll also fall behind everyone else.

I'm determined to turn things around so I get to work. I sprawl out on the rug in the center of the living room and start on my project. As I draw, I hear the front door open. Then I feel a gentle lick on my hand.

The pint-size slobber comes from Biscuit, my neighbor Linda's Chihuahua. He is brown and white with legs as wide as my thumb. Biscuit and Linda stay with me twice a week in the afternoons whenever Nick is at his summer job.

"Hi, Stella!" Linda says, shutting the front door. "Is my Biscuit bothering you?"

I shake my head.

"I think he just wants to see my drawing," I reply.

I like Biscuit because he is curious about everything. He often crawls from Linda's backyard through a tiny hole in our fence into our backyard. That's how we were first introduced to Biscuit ... and then Linda, when she came to get him.

"What fish are you drawing today?" Linda asks.

"A longnose butterflyfish. Did you know their design helps them blend into the coral reefs?"

"I did not," she replies. "Thank you for teaching me a new fact."

I pause.

"Linda, would you consider that a 'conversation starter'?"

She chuckles. "You know, I just might."

A conversation starter is what Mom calls a fun fact you can share when you're chatting with a new friend. I'm collecting them in my composition book for when I start fourth grade at the end of summer.

It'll help if I'm feeling quiet. Although I may not even need them, especially after what happened last school year with my new friend Stanley.

Stanley is one of my newest friends. When I first met him, I thought no way would he want to be friends with me. He is extroverted and I can be shy. Not to mention I acted like a total klutz in front of him on his first day! Turns out, I was very wrong. We've got a bunch in common and now we're close buddies.

Sadly, Stanley is gone for most of the summer on probably the most exciting adventure of everyone I know. He's in Texas visiting family and going to his own amazing summer camp: NASA Space Camp. He is going to be a Junior Space Explorer for a whole week! He's going to learn about gravity, program a robot, and maybe even explore a space rocket. I'd rather explore the oceans than outer space. I get motion sickness and those rockets shooting out into space make me queasy. But there is no denying that Stanley is going to have one of the coolest experiences known to humankind.

Summer would definitely be more exciting if Stanley weren't away. If Stanley were here, he'd be learning about marine animals with me. He loves the aquarium almost as much as I do. Instead he's having an epic adventure while I'm just sitting here at home. He promised to email me with his dad's email account, but I'm afraid he's going to be too busy to remember.

I sigh and look at my drawing.

"If only I could do something big this summer, too."

Chapter Three

As the afternoon progresses, I move on from drawing to reading. The book I'm reading now is the greatest. It's from the library, and it's about Sylvia Earle. She's a marine biologist and the first female chief scientist for the U.S. National Oceanic and Atmospheric Administration. Lately she's been working to save the oceans through her organization Mission Blue. Reading about her makes me think that girls like me can accomplish big things.

I close my eyes and daydream of exploring the ocean when I hear *jingle-jingle. Clackety-clack.*

I perk up. The sound of keys and high heels lets me know Mom is home. I run toward her.

"Hi, Perla," Linda says to Mom. It's always weird hearing people call Mom by her first name.

"Hi, Linda. Looks like you're finishing another fabulous project."

Linda smiles as she holds up a Chihuahua-size sweater that she is knitting. Mom wraps her arm around my shoulder.

"*Hola, mi inteligentísima hija*," Mom says. "What amazing things did you learn today?"

So much, I think, but then I remember the absolute, most fascinating thing. I grab my other book and flip to a page.

"Did you know there is a volcano in Antarctica?"

"Wow!"

"It's on Deception Island!" I say, pointing to the picture of a black volcano surrounded by icy blue glaciers.

"*¡Increíble!* You know, talk of Antarctica puts me in the mood for ice cream. Want to go, *mi amor?*"

The day has certainly become exciting now that Mom is home.

As Linda grabs her tote bag in one hand and Biscuit in the other to leave, Mom asks her, "Linda, would you like us to bring you anything from Oberweis?"

Mom tried a few times to pay Linda for baby-sitting me twice a week, but Linda always refuses. She says that's because she loves my company and "that's payment enough." Still, Mom insists on giving her a little something every time.

"One scoop of vanilla with a cake cone on the side, please. Biscuit just loves a bite of the cone."

Biscuit barks. I can't tell if it's because Linda said his name or if he really wants a cake cone. Either way, by the wiggle of his tail, he looks delighted. Mom changes quickly into her comfy clothes and we head to our local ice cream shop.

"What ice cream flavor are you going to get today?" I ask Mom as we walk down the street. I'm practically skipping. With her being so busy at work, it feels like a special treat to be able to hang out with her.

"*No sé*. I need some inspiration."

Mom insists inspiration is important. It's what gives you an idea or sparks your imagination. For Mom, inspiration at Oberweis comes from sampling a few flavors.

Right after I order my favorite, lime sherbet with nuts, Mom is immediately inspired. After one look at Cappuccino Chocolate Chunk, she is convinced. I'm digging a giant spoonful of lime sherbet when Mom says, "I've got some exciting news for *mi estrellita*. An email."

My eyes grow big.

"Stanley?"

Mom shakes her head. "No, but still very exciting! We heard back—"

I interrupt her. "Is it what I think it is?"

She nods. "You've been accepted into the Shedd Aquarium summer camp."

I almost drop my ice cream as I squeeze Mom with both arms.

"When does it start? It's not too much money?" My mind is filled with questions.

"A little over a month from now, and not at all. Especially since I saved up for it."

I exhale.

"I'm so proud of you, Stella," she says, patting my head.

I grin. Mom is proud of me just like she is of Nick. Better yet, I finally have my own adventure for this summer.

Chapter Four

After dropping off Linda's ice cream, Mom and I play cards, our Friday night tradition, until Nick comes home from work. Covered in splotches of marinara sauce, Nick walks in smelling like yummy garlic. These are the perks of his part-time job at a pizza restaurant. That and the occasional breadsticks.

"*Hola!*" he says, tossing his name tag onto the counter. I notice that it says NICOLAS instead of Nick. I hold the name tag in my hands like evidence in a detective show.

"Nicolas?" I point at the name tag. "But you go by Nick."

I don't bother to mention that I used to call him Kiki. That's when I was really little and couldn't pronounce his name.

"Oh, they just made the name tag based on my application. I thought I'd try it out. Sounds kind of cool."

"Weird," I reply.

He messes up my curls. "You're weird."

Mom chuckles. "How was work, *niño*?"

"Fun. My friend John and I did a competition to see who could make the most pizzas tonight. He barely won."

Nick starts stretching. He's been taking karate classes. That is one reason he has a part-time job. He wanted to pay for them. Because of the classes, he stretches all the time. The bigger reason is that Nick wants to save up money to buy a car one day. It sounds very impressive and hard. He's going to have to make many pizzas. I've seen game shows and I know how expensive cars can be.

"Well, I found out that I'm going to the Shedd Aquarium summer camp," I say proudly.

"Way to go, sis!" Nick replies, while trying to do splits.

Standing back up, Nick says, "Mom, I was thinking."

"Yes?"

"Do you think I could start driving lessons soon? I'll be fifteen next month. I'm going to need to learn how to drive if I'm going to get a car."

"*Posiblemente*. Let's see how much they are."

I look at Mom. She quietly gulps. I bet she's thinking the same thing I am. Nick is turning fifteen years old. That sounds so old. Not as old as my *abuelo*, but pretty grown-up.

"But why do you need to drive?" I ask. "You can walk and ride your bike."

"Yeah, but then I could drive us to school or maybe do pizza delivery. There are some older kids at the shop who do that. They say they make even more

17

money delivering than just making pizzas. Especially delivering at the big houses."

Nick then pretends to drive with a couch pillow as his steering wheel. "*Vroom, vroom*," he says, dashing around the living room. "See, I'd be a great driver."

I roll my eyes. He's not that mature.

Nick looks over at me and winks. "Want a ride?"

He gives me a piggyback ride around the living room. I laugh so hard that I can barely breathe as he zips around. I guess it's good that Nick isn't too mature to have fun. When he drops me off on the couch, he adds, "Don't forget to rate me and give a big tip!"

"Five stars," I reply, still giggling.

Before going to bed, I go up to Pancho in my room. He swims in his fishbowl happily when he sees me.

"I'm glad I don't have to worry about you changing or wanting to be named Francisco instead of Pancho. You always stay the same."

I turn off the lights.

"*Buenas noches*, my fish friend."

Chapter Five

I wake up the next morning to the sound of the vacuum. It's a terrible noise, especially when you are trying to sleep. It's noise pollution for my ears. Whenever I think of noise pollution, I feel bad for the whales. All the noise that people make in the ocean with their boats and oil rigs is driving them crazy! Unfortunately, the noise also stresses them out and makes them sick. Scientists say that may be a reason why whales are beaching themselves more often.

Thinking of the whales makes me sad, and it's too early to feel sad. Also, I have no plans of getting out of bed, so I cover my face with my blanket to drown out the noise. The door squeaks open.

"Oh, are you still sleeping?"

Mom has the vacuum in her hand. Through the holes of my blanket, I spy that she has a sly smile.

"*Perdoname*," she says, asking for forgiveness. I feel her sit down next to me on the bed, and she starts singing "*Duérmete, niña.*" I angrily throw off the blankets.

"First of all, '*Duérmete, niña*' is for sleepy time." I sit up in bed and cross my arms. "Not to mention it's a song for night and it's now morning."

She laughs and kisses the top of my head.

"Okay, okay. I'm awake," I say. It's hard to be too upset with Mom.

"Buenos días, mi Stellita."

I swing my legs around the bed. I rub my eyes trying to get the sleep out.

"You got an email from Stanley."

I leap out of bed.

"Why didn't you start with that?"

Mom puts her hand to her chest.

"Perdoname."

Over *pan tostado*, Mom and I read Stanley's email together on the computer.

Mom moves the mouse around for me because my fingers are sticky from the jam on my toast.

> *Hola*, Stella!
>
> How are you? I'm doing great. My dad
> and I just went to West Texas for a
> quick trip before my NASA Space Camp.
> It's so different from the rest of Texas.
> There are cacti and mountains. I even

saw a jackrabbit! The best part is I saw not just one real-life telescope, but three! They were enormous and weigh a ton! I'd say they're almost the size of a school bus. It was at the McDonald Observatory. The tour guide let me move it with this remote control. It was so cool! I feel officially ready now for my space camp. I mean, who else there will have operated a real-life telescope?

What about you? Are you doing anything fun? Let me know!

Sincerely,
Stanley

"Sounds like he is having a great time," Mom says.

"Vacations are the best," I reply.

Mom nods.

"They are also inspiring." I nudge Mom with my elbow.

Mom chuckles. "Well maybe we could go on our own little vacation before your camp starts."

I nod enthusiastically.

"I've been looking into visiting family. I'm just waiting to hear back from work if I can take the time off," she says.

I squeal. I wonder where we would go. Tía Maria might be traveling somewhere cool in the United States. Maybe we'll join her! One summer we drove to see her in Washington, D.C. We visited all the sites, like the Air and Space Museum and the Capitol. If this vacation were to happen, then I will have two huge adventures this summer!

"Let me work on it. But first, do you want help replying back to Stanley?"

I pause and stare at the keyboard keys. I pull at my curls. My summer hasn't been nearly as interesting as his yet. I only just found out about my summer camp, but I have nothing else to add beyond that.

I turn toward Mom. "I don't know what to write."

"Well, you don't have to write back right away. This email is going to stay magically in the computer until you're ready," she says, tapping the screen. "Maybe Jenny's party will give you some inspiration."

I hug Mom. She's so smart.

"And by the look of the clock, you should probably go get ready," she says, putting the vacuum up in the closet.

I'm excited to see Jenny. I haven't seen her as much as I'd like since she started her dance camp. This should be extra fun too since it's a party.

At Jenny's family parties, I'm the only non-Vietnamese person there and many of them prefer speaking Vietnamese. I really don't mind it at all. It's less pressure than when I'm visiting my own family. At my family events, I have so much I want to say, but I don't have all the Spanish words I want to say to them. This time, I am determined to try to learn a little Vietnamese and be a better party guest.

When I get in Jenny's mom's car, I ask right away. "How do you say hello in Vietnamese?"

Jenny sighs. "It's complicated."

"What do you mean?"

"Well, it depends whether the person you're speaking to is younger, older, much older, a boy or if they are a girl."

Scratch that, I think. There is no way I can memorize that many ways to say *hola*. Then I have another great idea.

"What about thank you?"

"It's sort of the same. You have to make it special for each person," she replies.

I gulp. "I'll just smile."

"Good idea," says Jenny's mom, giving me the thumbs-up in the mirror.

"How is dance camp going?" I say, switching topics. I really want to tell her about my Shedd summer camp, but I figure it's polite to ask her about her camp first.

"Awesome." Jenny beams. "Ms. Charlton is going to assign parts for the big recital soon. I can't wait to hear what part I get."

I quiver. The idea of performing in front of that many people still sounds a little scary. Not for Jenny, though. Jenny can sing, dance, and talk in front of anyone. If she were a fish, she would definitely not be a sargassum fish. They look like seaweed with eyes and hide among the seagrass beds. Jenny is happy to stand out. She is more like a brightly colored mantis shrimp.

Now it's my turn to share my amazing news.

"Super cool!" Jenny replies after I tell her about my camp. "I hope you get to pet a dolphin."

"Me too!"

When we arrive at the house party, it looks almost like the Vietnamese New Year's party we went to last year. Until Jenny, I didn't realize that Vietnamese people had their own New Year. That party was amazing because it was during the day, not night, and we ate from a giant buffet. But this party is a graduation celebration for Jenny's cousin Michelle, who just graduated from college.

"Is this your whole family?" I ask Jenny, looking at a packed room.

She laughs. "Nah. Some of the people are from my mom and auntie's temple."

Even though I can't speak back to everyone at the party, I make sure to smile very big. It seems to work because people smile back and share more delicious food. I even make sure to say "thank you" clearly like my speech teacher, Ms. Thompson, taught me. To my surprise, a few people reply "you're welcome" without any accent at all. It makes me turn a little *roja* like a tomato. I guess they're just like Mom's friends from work who can speak English well, but prefer to speak their language with friends and family. When we see Michelle, we make sure to chat with her.

"I made you a graduation card," I say.

"I love it," she replies, carefully examining my narwhal drawing. I wanted to draw her a squirrelfish, but I thought she might not know what one was. While the squirrelfish are pretty cute-looking with gigantic eyes, narwhals are a crowd favorite.

"So are you moving back?" Jenny asks eagerly. Michelle is Jenny's favorite cousin and used to baby-sit her when Jenny's mom was at work.

"Not yet. I'm taking a gap year," Michelle replies excitedly.

"What's that?" I ask.

"A year to explore and help the world before I have to work full-time."

"WOW!" I reply, practically jumping off the ground.

Michelle giggles. "I'm going to volunteer at the Marine Mammal Center near San Francisco. I'll be able to help rehabilitate otters, seals, and other types of animals."

My mouth drops open. The idea of saving sea critters sounds amazing. It also sounds like the perfect job for me.

"It's important for everyone to play a part in taking care of the earth. After all, we only have one planet. Can you imagine how much better the environment would be if we all chipped in?"

Before I can ask Michelle more about her gap year, she gets pulled into another conversation. Jenny and I head to the buffet for yummy food.

While we eat pork and rice dumplings, I notice people giving Michelle all these red envelopes. They sparkle with gold drawings on top.

"Do we get one?" I ask, leaning over to Jenny.

"Those are only for Michelle."

"Why?"

She whispers, "They're full of money."

I begin to exclaim, "Whoa, but I want one . . . ," but Jenny hushes me.

"You only get red envelopes on big days like your graduation or a wedding."

Jenny looks at me. I must look disappointed, because she says, "I know. I just can't wait till my graduation. I keep trying to convince my mom every year to give me a graduation party. Maybe fifth grade. Cross your fingers."

I slurp up more rice noodles from my bowl of pho and turn to Jenny.

"This is a two-thumbs-up party. Thank you for bringing me."

"I can't go to a party without my best friend." Jenny throws her arm around me.

After we stuff ourselves with food, we play tag in the backyard with the only other kids from the party.

Then we run back inside to eat sweet rice dumplings stuffed with mung bean paste. By that point, the party is getting louder. Some of the parents are even singing karaoke! Most of the kids we were playing tag with run back outside in embarrassment at the sight of their parents singing, but Jenny and I stay inside to watch the show. I could never sing in front of a crowd, but it's fun to watch other people do it.

On the car ride home, I start thinking of all the stellar things I have to write to Stanley, especially about Michelle. I want to save the world, too—especially sea creatures. And I don't want to wait till after college. At the rate summer is going, that's way too far away.

Chapter Six

Dear Stanley,

I can't wait till my summer camp. I hope I get to feed the penguins at least once. I'm really hoping they will give me one, too, but I don't think that is realistic.

I also looked into the Marine Mammal Center where Michelle is going to volunteer. And guess what I learned? The animals in the oceans are in danger! There are sea lions that get injured by boats or wrapped up in fishing nets. Thankfully, some of them get rescued and go to the Mammal Center to be rehabilitated. But still, this is a real problem. I wish there was something I could do right now to prevent it!

I'm contemplating something else to write to Stanley when Mom comes home from work.

"Where's your *hermano*?" she says, looking

annoyed for a second. I'm not supposed to be on the computer alone. I flash a little guilty smile.

"He's in his room. He was with me, but then he got a phone call. I'm about to finish my email."

The phone call Nick got was a little strange. When I picked up the phone, I heard a person's voice I didn't recognize. It sounded like a girl. She also asked for Nicolas, not Nick.

"*Ni modo*." Mom flips her hand and leans in. "I can tell you the good news first."

It must be enormously good. Her face can hardly contain the excitement.

"Pack your *maletas*. We're going to *México*!" Mom says in a singsong voice.

I scream. We've only been back to Mexico once since we moved here, but I was four years old and barely remember anything.

"REALLY? I'm going to go pack my bags right now." I dash toward my room. I'm waving my arms around chanting, "Mexico, Mexico."

"*Cálmate*, Stella. Let's eat some dinner and then you can start packing."

I stop mid run. I pause and then ask, "Can I at least start making a list?"

She walks over to me and kisses the top of my head.

"*Claro que sí.* Let's go tell your brother."

Nick's reaction to the fabulous news, as usual, is more reserved than mine. He says, "Cool."

"Well, we think it's very cool, too." She puts her hands on her hips.

"Super cool!" I say, throwing my arms around him.

Nick groans. "Ugh . . . but . . ."

I let go of him.

"What's wrong?" Mom asks.

"What about my job?" he replies.

"It's only a few days, *niño*." Mom sighs. "You won't be missing much work, and it's important to visit family."

"I guess so," he replies, crossing his arms and

muttering, "Nobody ever checks with me first what I want to do."

Mom looks a little upset.

"I'm sorry that I didn't check with you first about going on a fabulous vacation."

Nick looks embarrassed. "I'll let the pizzeria know, it shouldn't be a problem."

Mom grabs my hand. "*Vámonos, niñita*. Let's make dinner. And our list of things to pack."

Mom makes *arroz con frijoles* for dinner. While rice and beans doesn't sound extraordinary, it simply is. It also takes a long time to make. Mom picks up one of the beans that's she has been soaking overnight and pinches it. The single *frijole* melts like butter in her hand.

"*¡Perfecto!*"

She then grabs a yellow box from the cabinet and laughs. Mom's holding the KNORR CHICKEN SEASONINGS box. The box is labeled both in English and Spanish.

"Remember when you used to call this 'chicken de *pollo*?'"

I turn *roja*. I basically was calling it "chicken of chicken." To be fair, those are the two biggest words on the box.

Mom sees my reaction.

"Don't be embarrassed, *mi amor*. That was adorable."

Whenever Mom pokes fun at my Spanish, it usually never bothers me. This time, though, it reminds me that I don't speak *español muy bien*. Gulp. And we're going to Mexico. Soon.

"Mom?"

"*¿Sí, Stella?*"

"Do you think we can read one of those Spanish books Maria gave me tonight?"

My *tía* Maria is constantly giving me picture books to practice my Spanish. Sometimes I try reading them out loud, but I usually give up after a page. My head starts hurting from having to think about what every word and every letter sounds like. Plus, I get confused if I'm pronouncing the way I should in

English or Spanish. The problem is the letters are similar, but the way you pronounce some of the letters is very different. On top of that, my tongue feels heavy in my mouth like it's swollen up and can't move right. Even if I make it through a few pages, I usually want to take a *siesta* afterward from thinking too much. But if we're going to Mexico, I better try *un poquito*. I know what I have to do.

"And . . . Mom?" I notice my voice sounds higher pitched than normal.

"*Sí, Stella*," she replies as she dices up garlic.

"Can you only speak Spanish, too? Just for a little bit."

"*Solamente español, sí.*"

Since Mom's hands are busy, she kisses the top of my head. Hearing Mom speak Spanish makes me less nervous about Mexico. Like usual, I can understand everything she is saying. If I can understand her, then I should be okay.

As she continues to cook, Mom names the things we need to pack in *español*.

"*Traje de baño*," she says.

I write down "swimsuit."

"*Zapatos.*"

I write down "shoes."

"*Cepillo de dientes.*"

I write down "toothbrush."

"*Calzones.*"

I giggle and write down "underwear."

We continue with our list until dinner is ready. Nick emerges from his room to join us.

At the table, Mom switches back to speaking mostly English by accident, and I don't stop her. I feel tired from listening to each word carefully.

As we dig in, Nick begins to ask questions about the trip.

"When are we going?"

Mom wipes her mouth with a napkin. "Very soon. We're going to celebrate your birthday there."

"That's in two weeks," I exclaim, dropping my fork. "And then when we get back, it's my summer camp!"

Mom smiles. "Yes, the timing was perfect! The

Aeromexico plane tickets were on special for those dates. So I can take off from work, and you don't have to miss any camp. It's *perfecto*!"

Nick sulks a little.

"It's not perfect for me, though." Then he adds, "What about my birthday party with my friends?"

"*Te prometo* as soon as we get back you can do something fun with your friends," Mom replies. She looks more disappointed that Nick isn't as excited.

"I guess. Well, are we going to Mexico City?" he replies, staring at his plate of food.

Mom furrows her eyebrows at Nick.

"Not this time. We're going to stay with Tía Maria in Oaxaca. She has that big house that we can all stay in and have never been to. We might be able to go to the beach, too."

"The ocean!" I squeal. I look over at Nick. He is still pushing around his rice and beans with his fork.

Nick should be excited about the beach! The only beach we have in Chicago is on Lake Michigan, and it's too cold to swim there most of the year. Believe it or not, I've never set foot on an ocean beach. I know it's going to be a "life-changing" experience. That's what Jacques Cousteau and Sylvia Earle both said about their first experiences in the ocean.

"Any more questions?" Mom asks, looking warily at Nick.

Then I think of a good one.

"Who is going to take care of Pancho?" I ask.

"I'll ask Linda. If she can't, I'll take him to the office. Everyone will love him."

Then it occurs to me that I might have a problem.

"How will I write to Stanley?"

"We will have email there, but I was also thinking. What if you write letters? Like pen pals?"

I am intrigued, but that does seem like a lot of work. Plus, letters can take days to get somewhere! When we press send on the computer, Stanley receives my email right away, like magic. Mom can tell just by looking at me that I'm not sold on it.

"Writing letters *es muy divertido*. You can include drawings and you won't have to worry about using my email or waiting to use the computer." Mom makes a very eager expression.

I am a little more convinced. Stanley does like my drawings.

"Did you know I had a pen pal with a girl from London when I was a teenager?" says Mom.

"Really?" I reply.

"Do you know how exciting it was to get a letter from another country?"

My eyes grow wide. I bet Stanley will freak out if he gets a letter from Mexico and thinks I'm having the best summer. "Okay, I'll do it!"

Mom looks relieved. I think she may not want me using her email as much. The three emails this week might have been too many.

"Now," I say, "let's get back to our things-to-pack list."

I write down "pen and paper" and think about all the adventures I'll be writing to Stanley.

Chapter Seven

The next morning, I write my first handwritten letter to Stanley asking if he wants to be pen pals this summer. I make sure to include my address. I suspect he knows where I live since we've ridden bikes together, but better to be safe than sorry.

"You're not going to include anything about Mexico?" asks Nick. He's standing by the kitchen counter, snacking again. He's already finished a bowl of cereal. Now, he's carefully unwrapping individual cheese slices and stuffing them into his mouth one at a time. Mom says teenagers need to eat often because their bodies are growing fast, but

I think he must be growing extra fast by the amount he eats.

"I think I want to keep the trip a secret. I'm sure he'll flip out once he finds out."

"Sneaky, sis." He taps my forehead.

"Nick, can you tell me about Mexico again?"

"Why do you want to hear it from me? You'll see it soon enough."

He looks annoyed. I don't know why Nick is so moody now. When we were younger, Nick used to love to tell me stories about our *abuelo*'s house and playing in Chapultepec. I miss his long stories about the park full of palm trees and a castle.

"Fine. I'll ask Dad," I reply, pouting. "He remembers more than you anyway."

"Whatever," says Nick, walking away with another cheese slice in hand.

Dad lives in Colorado and usually calls once a week. My parents divorced when I was five. He's not always the best dad, like he sometimes forgets to call or makes promises that he doesn't keep. But he's not all bad, and I know he tries the best that he can. This week, fortunately, he remembers to call. That's great, too, because I have many questions to ask him about Mexico, like the weather, what our old house was like, and of course Oaxaca.

When I finally tell him about our trip, he replies, "*¡Qué bueno!* You're going to love Oaxaca, Stella."

"Is there anything I should do while we're there, *Papá*?"

"You should eat the *chapulines*."

"What are those?"

"I won't tell you." Then he adds, "It will be *una rica sorpresa*."

I'm cautious. Dad surprises aren't always as great as Mom surprises. They are usually little disappointments more than anything, like the time he surprised us by introducing us to his new girlfriend, but I'm willing to give it a try.

The remaining days till our vacation zoom by, and before I know it, we're heading on our trip. I make sure to pack my ocean books, journals, drawing materials, and sunscreen. I try to jam more books in my backpack before the taxi arrives.

"We're only going for five days, *niña*," says Mom.

"I just want to make sure I'm ready for my first ocean experience. It's my job as a future Shedd Aquarium camper."

Mom laughs. "Okay, one more book."

Nick rolls his eyes and I give him a hard stare.

On the taxi ride to O'Hare airport, I double-check my to-do list. Only two items remain:

- Stanley's Address
- Passports

I put check marks next to both. Stanley's dad emailed Mom their address yesterday, and Mom triple-checked our passports. I ask Mom if I can hold the passports in the taxi, but she says they are too important. Mom lets me look at them instead. On the front it says ESTADOS UNIDOS MEXICANOS. As I touch the lovely green cover, I wonder about the United States part.

"Mom? How many states are there in Mexico?"

"Thirty-one and one federal district. Mexico City is like Washington, D.C. It is its own tiny state. That's why we used to call it D.F., *Distrito Federal*, but it recently changed. Now we just call it *la Ciudad de México*."

Suddenly, I feel butterflies in my stomach. Even though Mexico is my home, I realize there is so much I don't know about it. Once we're on the airplane, my butterflies double in size when I hear the overhead announcements in Spanish. Is everything going to be only in *español*? I breathe a sigh of relief when they repeat them in English.

"Whoa, there is a TV," says Nick, elbowing me. It's the most excited he's sounded all morning.

"See, there's a documentary on the oceans and some animated movies," he says and then hands me a pair of headphones. I clap my hands with joy.

My nerves are completely gone once the snacks are served on the flight. They serve us these packages of zesty *cacahuates japoneses*. I don't quite understand why a Mexican airline hands out Japanese peanuts as a snack, but I'm not complaining. They are crunchy, salty, and superb!

When the flight attendant checks on us, I try practicing my Spanish. I want to ask her when the flight lands, but it doesn't go so well. She speaks so fast; I can't understand her. I think I heard the word *agua*, but I'm not sure. I turn *roja*.

"Do you want some water?" she asks again, this time in English.

I reply softly, "*Si, por favor.*"

I look at Mom. My stomach is feeling a little uneasy again.

"How come I can always understand you?"

"It's okay, *Stellita*. There are some people I can't understand in Spanish either."

"Really?"

"Don't get me started!" she replies, laughing.

I tilt my head at her in confusion.

"It's complicated. There are many Spanish-speaking countries, and each country has its own unique words. Like in Spain, they call a pen a *bolígrafo*, but in Mexico we call it a *pluma*. If I'm speaking with someone from Chile, for example, and they use words that I'm not familiar with, I can get confused. It happens to all of us."

Hearing that Mom struggles sometimes with Spanish makes me feel a little better.

Though the flights are long and we have a layover, I'm not tired at all when we land in Oaxaca. In fact, I feel all tingly with excitement. It bubbles over when I see my *tía* Maria. Maria is the easiest of my relatives to talk to. She speaks so many languages, not to mention English, perfectly.

She welcomes us with hugs and kisses. "*¡Bienvenidos!*"

She looks at us and shakes her head. "*Qué bonitos*,

but you all look too skinny. Let's go home quick, and I will feed you."

Exiting the airport, I can feel the heat on my face. It's so much warmer here than in Chicago. I also don't hear a single word of English outside of Maria and Mom. Some of the Spanish I can understand perfectly, but some of it doesn't make sense! It's a little overwhelming, so I hold on to Mom's hand tighter. The streets are also littered with those bug Volkswagen cars. I immediately start tapping

Nick with my free hand. "Slug bug white. Slug bug taxi."

He looks a little annoyed. "Kiddo. There are a bunch of them here. You're going to get tired of this game if you keep it up."

I look out the window. "I'll take a break then."

Then I whisper softly, "For now."

Chapter Eight

In comparison to the airport, Tía Maria's
home feels quiet and peaceful. It's also very different
from our place in Chicago. Maria's house stands by
itself on a big piece of land surrounded by moun-
tains, and it is painted red. Our place is brick and
only a few feet from our neighbors. Her house looks
like an old *hacienda*, and ours is just a house. I touch
the walls of her home with my hands. It doesn't feel
like brick.

"It's made of *adobe*," Maria says.

"*What's that?*" I ask.

"*Adobe* is a house made out of

mud and other natural materials. When it dries, it's as strong as brick," she says. "It helps the house stay naturally cooler in the summer. People have been making houses this way for thousands of years."

My mouth drops.

"Let's drop off your *maletas*, and then I'll take you around."

After we leave off our bags in the big guest room, Maria takes us on a tour of her home.

The walls are covered with pictures of her from her adventures. Each picture is more impressive than the next.

"This is at the United Nations." She points at one picture. "When I was on a women's rights committee."

I'm not quite sure what the United Nations is, but it sounds awfully important. Especially anything related to women's rights. I learned in Ms. Bell's class that women haven't always had the same rights as men. The fact that Maria was on a committee for them means she must be a special person.

"Amazing," I reply.

"It's important to me to make sure that you and all women have the opportunity to be and do whatever you want," she says, looking at me with her bright green eyes.

Then I see a framed picture of Maria sitting on some rocks next to the beach. She looks much younger, but there is the same sparkle in her eyes.

"And this picture is from Barcelona when I was teaching at the university out there."

"Wow," I reply. It's all I can say. She must be super smart, too. She's like my own personal Sylvia Earle.

"I hope you brought your swimsuit." She winks. "We'll go to the beach in a day or two."

I nod enthusiastically.

Then I run up to Mom and squeeze her hand.

"I'm excited, too," she says, taking the words out of my mouth.

"And I'm hungry," Nick adds.

Maria takes us into the historic part of Oaxaca

City for dinner. It's easy to tell that it's old because the streets are cobbled. The buildings are also brightly painted red, orange, and yellow. The plazas are filled with plants and *artesanos* selling their crafts. As we pass other people on the street, I notice many of their faces look like mine. This makes me more than ever want to fit in, like I belong in the place where I was born. So, when I find a postcard for Stanley, I ask Mom if I can buy it by myself. Mom gives me the change so I can pay the vendor ten pesos.

We don't say much, but I make sure to start with "*hola*" and end with "*muchas gracias.*" To which he replies, "*De nada, señorita.*"

I skip back to Mom, who gives me the thumbs-up. A tiny step in the right direction, I think. Then we continue on our walk.

Maria leads us through a doorway to a secret restaurant. Well, it's not really a secret, but it's hidden from the street. You have to go between two stores into a beautiful courtyard to find the restaurant.

"It's called *Las Danzantes*," Maria says.

"Does that mean 'the dancers'?" asks Nick.

"Yes! Very good, Nicolas," says Maria.

Weird, I think. This is the third time this summer I've heard him called Nicolas. I wonder if I can still call him Nick.

My stomach rumbles and I focus on the more pressing issue—dinner. As I look at the menu, I think I can understand half of the words.

Like *postre*, which means dessert. Yes, *por favor*.

Verduras is mostly good. I like most vegetables. Although not eggplant. Eww.

"Can we try the *chapulines*?" I ask Maria, pointing to the menu.

She looks impressed. "Of course. They're a delicacy." She then says, "If you eat them, you'll be a true *Mexicana*."

I quickly realize that it doesn't matter what is on the menu. Because of Maria, we're being treated like special guests. Maria has been living in Oaxaca for most of her adult life and knows everyone. The owner even comes out to say hello to us. He hugs and kisses her and says a few things I can't understand. My eyes start to glaze over. Finally, he looks at me and says more slowly, *"Tu tía es una mujer muy importante."*

"You must take after me," Mom says to Maria, winking.

If the owner of a restaurant says Maria is very important, then she really must be. I think about the amazing women in my family. Hopefully I can grow up to be like them one day.

As requested, we get an order of *chapulines*. When I see them, I'm immediately not a fan. Neither is Nick.

"Grasshoppers?!" we exclaim.

"*No se preocupes, niños*. Let me show you."

Maria scoops a few into a corn tortilla and adds avocado and pickled onions. She hands it to me.

I grab it hesitantly from her. I stare for a few seconds. I can hear Maria's and Dad's voices echoing in my head how "they're a delicacy" and how I'm a true *Mexicana* if I eat it.

I close my eyes. I squinch my face, but I slowly take a bite. It's crunchy, but it's also very salty and tastes like lime.

"Yum!" I say. I'm not lying either. It's *delicioso*!

With our stomachs full of food, we head back to Maria's and drift off to sleep in one giant room on different cots. I feel electric and still a little nervous. I'm so happy to be in Mexico, but I also wish that I wake up tomorrow fluent in Spanish. Before I shut my eyes, I whisper, "Thank you, Mom, for the vacation."

Nick whispers, "Yeah, Mom." I think I spot a smile on his face.

"You're welcome, *niños*," Mom replies with an even bigger smile.

Chapter Nine

It's not till the third day of our vacation that we finally make it to the beach. I could hardly sleep the night before in anticipation of my first seaside experience.

"Are you excited, Mom?" I whisper to her in the morning after the alarm clock rings. It's super early. So early that it's still dark outside. We're in the same time zone as Chicago, so it's probably still dark at home, too. I bet Jenny, Linda, and Biscuit are still asleep. The fact that the sun isn't up yet doesn't matter to me. I'm ready to get our day started.

"Of course. I love the beach," she says, yawning. "I can't wait to share it with you."

We packed up the car the night before so we're able to hit the road right away after some papaya and breakfast *tamales*. Maria drives the car since she knows the way. Mom and I sit in the back seat while Nick drags himself in a sleepy daze to the front seat. His legs are getting too long for the back. He falls asleep right away.

After an hour the sun finally rises. "Only three more hours," I exclaim.

Now, four hours in the car can seem like a long time normally, but when you've been waiting your whole life to see the ocean, it's *nada*!

I try reading to make the time pass by, but I get queasy on the winding roads. Thankfully, Mom opens the window to make me feel better. She also reads aloud from a Sylvia Earle biography to distract me. The combination of her soothing voice and the cool breeze helps me feel nearly perfect.

"She's a fascinating woman!" Mom says, holding the book in her lap. Turns out, Sylvia Earle founded something called Hope Spots around the world through her organization Mission Blue. These are spots where no fishing or drilling is permitted. The idea is they can help preserve the oceans and offset some of the pollution.

As we get closer to the beach, the air begins to smell salty. It's more noticeable than I ever imagined. Though I'm surprised, it makes sense. The amount of salt in the oceans could cover the whole planet fifty meters deep.

On the horizon, I see a little strip of blue. At first, I think the blue might be the sky, but it shimmers. When I'm sure, I shout with delight, *"¡El océano!"*

"Calm down, kiddo, it's still early," Nick groans, shifting around the front seat.

"Which ocean is it?" I whisper to Mom, ignoring Nick.

"El Pacífico. You know, you've been here before."

"Really?" I reply, confused.

"You saw it when I was pregnant with you."

"That doesn't count. I was in there," I say, pointing to her belly.

"*¡Claro que cuenta!*" She wraps her arms around me.

The strip of blue grows and grows on the horizon as we get closer. Finally, Maria pulls the car into the hotel parking lot.

As soon as we are parked, we walk through the hotel. Mom and Maria want to look around the lobby, but all I want to do is go outside. I tug at Mom's arm impatiently.

"Okay, okay," Mom replies.

When we finally reach outdoors, I dart toward the beach. I rip off my sandals. The warm sand feels cozy under my toes. Then I stop. Staring face-to-face with the ocean for the first time, I'm speechless. It's huge! And lovelier than I ever imagined. Now I understand why people dedicate their entire lives to studying and protecting it.

I turn around. Everyone is happy, too. Even Nick is smiling. So much so, I can see all his teeth. This is the first time in a long time that I've seen him this happy.

Standing away from my family, I can fully see how much taller Nick has gotten. He is taller than both Mom and Maria! He turns fifteen soon, but it's the first time I notice he doesn't look like a kid.

"Nick, how do I get in?" I ask hesitantly. I love the ocean, but it's so big and wide that it makes me feel nervous to jump in.

Nick chuckles.

"You've just got to put in one foot at a time."

I cautiously walk up to the water while studying everything around me. There is an entire small world on the beach. There are shells that look just like the ones I've seen at the craft store. There are even itty-bitty hermit crabs scuttling around from spot to spot. As I get closer, I notice how the waves seem to say *hola* and *adiós* over and over. At first, I do almost a dance with the ocean. I walk toward the water when it goes "goodbye" and walk backward when the waves crash toward me saying "hi." I do that a few times until I see other kids my age just run in. They look so happy and unafraid. I pump my fists and say, "I can do this."

I finally move in each toe and wait for the next wave. I squeal with delight when the warm water rushes over my feet.

"See you've got it. Quick, try digging your feet in the sand before the next wave hits," Nick says.

With my feet stuck in, the wave flows over. I feel as if the ocean is pulling me in. I scream and look at Nick. He's in the same spot as before and so am I.

"We're not moving!"

"Cool isn't it?!" he replies, smiling.

I yell, "Mom come play with us."

"*Sí, sí, pero primero* sunblock."

Mom slathers us with sunscreen until our brown skin is chalky white and smells of coconuts. Then, with a nod of approval, the three of us run into the waves. It's easier to be brave with them by my side. I put on my goggles to see if I can see anything in the magical blue world below. On my first try, I see nothing and instead inhale salty water. I don't mind it one bit, although I do have to spit some water out. With some practice, I am able to catch a peek at a few tiny fishes and some seaweed.

"I want to do this all the time when I grow up," I whisper to myself.

After a little while, Mom decides to join Maria under a hotel umbrella on the beach.

"*Estoy cansada*. Have fun!" Mom says as she walks away.

A little later, Nick and I get tired of swimming, too, so we go exploring the beach. I scan everything with my eyes so I don't miss a thing. I spy seagulls and pelicans flying overhead. Over in the trees, I can see green birds with blue patches near their eyes and iguanas soaking in the sun. There are even

coconut shells in the sand. Then we discover, tucked away, a sea turtle nest! I've never seen one before in my life, but I can recognize it from my books. The nest has nearly a hundred white eggs covered with sand. The eggs are white like the color of toothpaste and the size of Ping-Pong balls. Part of me wants to grab one, but even though there are lots of them, I don't. As a new future Shedd summer camper, I know I mustn't. It's important to not disturb wildlife and never leave a trace. Plus, their Mom will miss them.

Standing near the nest is a scientist with red hair and freckles. At least I think he is a scientist, because he examines the eggs and places a sign around them.

"What are you doing?" asks Nick in Spanish.

"Just making sure the eggs are safe. We're protecting them from people," the man replies in Spanish, but with an American accent.

"Can I ask you a question?" I ask in English.

"Of course!" he replies. He looks relieved to be speaking English. I can relate!

"Why do they need protection? I can't imagine someone hurting them."

"Well, once their mom digs a hole for the nest, she lays her eggs and then returns to the ocean. Before she leaves, she does her best to protect it from predators by covering up the nest with sand. The problem is many people travel on this beach. It can be hard to notice the nest, especially if you're not paying attention. So I'm sure nobody means to hurt them, but sometimes people will accidentally trample on it with their feet or a vehicle. It's my job to make sure that doesn't happen. I'm watching out for these little guys while learning more about them."

I nod.

"I want to be a marine biologist," I tell him.

"That's great! Another person to care for our oceans!"

Suddenly I hear a new voice; it's a girl about my age. She's pulling her dad toward the sea turtles.

"Papá, mira. ¡Me encanta las tortugas!"

"*Yo también*," I reply, agreeing that I also love the sea turtles.

She speaks Spanish to me for a couple of minutes about the sea turtles. She does it at a normal pace so I'm able to understand her. Then she asks, "*¿De dónde eres?*"

I respond, "*Soy de* Chicago."

"*¡Qué triste!*"

She then explains why she is sad. She hoped that I might be a local like her so we could become friends.

I nod and secretly grin. A new friend is great, but I'm just happy that she saw me as someone from Mexico, too. Maybe I belong more than I think. We say our goodbyes to each other and wish the turtles good luck.

"*¡Buena suerte, bebés!*"

Chapter Ten

The last day of our trip is bittersweet.
We've had so much fun visiting other places in Oaxaca, like an ancient city with pyramids called *Monte Albán*. We also saw an art museum filled with *alebrijes* and textiles, until Nick said it was too boring. I don't want to leave Oaxaca, but I can't wait for camp to start either.

Today is also Nick's birthday. Because of our flight, it's a breakfast celebration at Maria's. While there is delicious cake with *cajeta*, I'd rather eat as much papaya and breakfast *tamales* as I can before we leave.

"*Tu regalo.*" Mom grins as she hands Nick a

birthday present. It's an envelope. Inside is an "I owe you" for driving lessons.

"We'll split the cost when you're ready to take classes."

Nick practically picks Mom off the ground.

Maria pats him on the back. *"Ahora, tu eres un hombre."* Nick blushes when Maria calls him a man. I quietly cross my arms in protest.

"I disagree," I mutter.

I feel a little nervous about giving Nick a handmade card and drawing after such a big gift, especially the way he's been acting lately. I never know if he is going to be happy or annoyed with things. Thankfully he loves it. My present is a drawing of the sea turtle nest we found and me as a scientist nearby.

"That's me when I'm older," I tell him.

He messes with my curls. "Obviously."

We get back to Chicago in the evening. It's a little hard to be back. I miss the warmer weather and my daily mango that was the color of the sun, but that sadness vanishes when we check the mail. There are two letters for me! There is a letter from Stanley and a letter from the Shedd with instructions for my first day at camp. Mom reads that while I carefully rip open the envelope from Stanley.

Hola, Stella!

I'd love to be pen pals! I read about it once in a book, and it seemed pretty neat. What have you been up to? I've been playing football with my cousins and going swimming almost every day. We went to this cool natural pool near their house called Barton Springs. The water was so cold! My teeth were chattering for, like, five minutes.

But best of all, I just finished my first day of Space Camp!!! All the kids at camp are cool, and we have a bunch in common. Today, we had to work in a group to program a robot! That was hard, but once it moved, it

was completely worth it. I haven't been in a
rocket ship yet, but they promise we'll explore
one soon. Write me back to tell me about
your adventures.

Sincerely,
Stanley!

This pen pal idea is brilliant. It's almost like an old spy movie. I wish I knew a secret code like pig latin or Morse code. Maybe I could try writing my entire letter backward so that Stanley can only read it in the mirror. Then I think that's too complicated. Instead, I settle for my sparkly pens and a piece of paper and write my letter. I tell him all about Mexico and my big plans.

When I finish, I drop my pen. I'm not sure how to end a letter. "Sincerely" sounds dull, especially after my trip.

"Mom, how do you end a letter in Spanish?"

"Well, in Spanish you'd say *atentamente*. Why?"

"I'm writing a letter back to Stanley. He does want to be pen pals this summer!"

Mom chuckles.

"I'd write *hasta pronto* since you will see him soon."

I scribble it down and sign the letter with my full name, Estrella Díaz. That's more proper. Mom promises to mail it tomorrow from work.

Next, Mom and I read the letter from the Shedd Aquarium. Turns out all I need is my journal, imagination, and some snacks. Then I start thinking about something Stanley wrote in his letter about the kids at his camp. I hadn't really thought about other kids who will be at my camp. I don't think I will know anyone there. Meeting new people can be a little scary.

"Mom, do you think there will be many kids at the camp?" I ask, trying not to look nervous.

"I don't know how many there will be, but I'm sure they will be nice. And I'm sure they will love the oceans just as much as you do."

I smile. That's true. Stanley also said everyone was nice at his camp. Then again, Stanley can make friends with anyone.

While Mom unpacks, I look at the Shedd envelope. There is a sea turtle on the front. It reminds me of the American scientist in Oaxaca and what he said about our oceans. Being a marine biologist is a big job, and if I'm going to protect the oceans, I'm going to need to learn how. I hope the people at the Shedd can help me.

Chapter Eleven

The night before my summer camp,
Nick has his birthday party with his friends. It turns
out to be a "private party." This exclusive event takes
place at the pizza shop with his best friend, Jason,
and a few of Nick's new work friends.

"You won't want to go," he tells me when he leaves
the house with Mom. "It's just a bunch of boys."

I feel a little hurt, but it does give me time to plan
my outfit for the first day of camp. I want to look
extra special. While I think I am a little less shy now
than last school year, I am still nervous the other
kids won't like me. So I need to dress to impress.
Biscuit and Linda help me decide on my favorite

polka-dot dress and an otter shirt on top. I know it's the best choice because Biscuit claps his paws when he sees the outfit all together.

I show it off as soon as Mom and Nick get home from the birthday *fiesta*.

"Can I sleep in my outfit? That way I'm ready just in case."

Mom shakes her head. "It'll get wrinkled. I also don't think you have to worry about being late. Knowing you, I'm more afraid you won't sleep much."

Mom was right. I end up checking my alarm clock almost every couple of hours. Part of it is that I'm excited, but I also keep thinking bad thoughts. Like what if there is someone like Jessica Anderson there? I think I can deal better with a bully now, but I don't want to be made fun of at all. Especially at one of my favorite places in the world.

In the morning, I ride into downtown with Mom

on the Metra. She's going to drop me off at the Shedd before work. It's always fun to ride the Metra, but it is so much busier on a Monday than it is on the weekends. The station stop is filled with *click clack* noises of high heels and dress shoes. I almost lose sight of Mom, but she grabs on to me tightly. Luckily, she finds me a seat on the train and stands, hovering over me.

I read a new letter from Stanley quietly before I tell Mom about it. I have to speak deep from my stomach, like I learned in speech class, for her to be able to hear me.

"Stanley got to explore a rocket ship! And, see, he even drew a little alligator at the bottom with a word bubble that says, 'See you later.'"

Mom smiles. "That's nice of him."

"I hope he gets my postcard and new letter soon."

After our Metra ride, we head over to the grassy fields toward the Shedd. With each step, my stomach starts twisting in knots. By the time we go up the stairs of the museum, I can feel the wave of *roja* coming on. I'm nervous. The words that came so easily to me on the Metra are gone.

Mom takes one look at me and knows that I'm getting nervous.

"You're going to be fine, *mi amor.*"

I try smiling, but it comes out weird like my face is frozen. Studying me, she puts her hand to my chin. She squints her eyes, looking for inspiration.

"I know what will help." She grabs a pen from her purse and draws a little star on the back of my hand.

"Una estrella."

Staring at my star, I take a deep breath.

She puts her hands on my shoulders.

"Estrella Díaz, my star, you'll be fine."

I look up at her and nod. Then we walk through the front revolving doors.

Chapter Twelve

In the lobby, we wait under Neptune's dome to check in. The large room makes me feel tiny.

"Did you know the same architectural firm that made this dome also made the domes at Wrigley Field and the Field Museum?" Mom says very proudly. "If you look closely, you can even see Neptune's trident." My mouth drops.

"I had to learn a few things to keep up with *mi inteligente* Stella." Mom winks.

I smile a little.

We're soon greeted by two adults wearing shirts that say CAMP COUNSELOR. One is an older man with some gray hairs. Beside him is a small brunette woman with short hair.

"Welcome! We're Mr. Kyle and Ms. Susan."

Ms. Susan bends down to me.

"And who might you be?"

"Stella Díaz," I reply softly.

"Stella Díaz! The future Jacques Cousteau, I hear." She checks my name off a list and hands me a badge to wear on my shirt.

I beam from ear to ear. I realize I'm surrounded by my people, my fellow sea creature enthusiasts.

"Actually, I think I might want to be Sylvia Earle now," I continue. "Did you know she, along with her husband, formed Deep

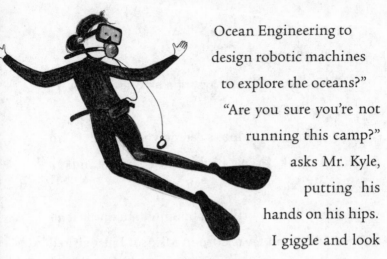

Ocean Engineering to design robotic machines to explore the oceans?"

"Are you sure you're not running this camp?" asks Mr. Kyle, putting his hands on his hips.

I giggle and look at Mom. She squeezes my shoulder.

"*Que te diviertas*," she whispers, telling me to have fun.

With a kiss on the head, Mom heads to work.

Mr. Kyle and Ms. Susan take me to a room where there are groups of other kids. The camp is for grades three through five, so no one is too much older. One girl smiles at me right away. She looks Latina with long, curly brown hair and tanned skin. She looks exactly like the friend I always wished who would be in my class. Someone like me who loves sea creatures. I'm excited when she comes up to me.

"I'm Mariel De La Cruz."

"I'm Stella Díaz."

"*¿Hablas español?*" she says, raising one eyebrow.

"*Un poquito,*" I reply.

She immediately looks let down. Quick! I can fix this, I think. I reply back, "But I understand! *Yo entiendo.*"

She still looks a little disappointed. In one last attempt I add, "And I was born in Mexico! I just visited my family there, too."

Her face softens some. It's hard sometimes being Mexican and not being able to speak Spanish well. I thought I had made some progress in Mexico, but now I feel like I just took two steps back.

I start feeling nervous. This isn't going as well as I'd hoped it would. Then another kid comes over. She has braids all over her head.

"Hi, I like your otter shirt. I'm Kristen."

"Thanks. I'm Stella."

"Do you know anyone here?" she asks.

I shake my head no.

"Me neither." As her face forms a smile, I can see a mouth full of braces. They have different brightly colored bands on each tooth. It looks like jewelry for her teeth.

"Let's stick together," she says.

I let out a giant exhale.

"Yes, please."

As we sit down next to each other, Mr. Kyle and Ms. Susan rise to stand in front of the group. Ms. Susan begins: "Looks like everyone is here. Let's have everyone stand up and introduce themselves. Make sure to mention something fun, too."

Kristen starts. She's very confident. Turns out she's going into fifth grade next school year. Seeing her go makes me want to try to go next. I've been trying to pretend I'm brave. *Fake it until you make it*, they say. *I'm just nervous because I care*, they say.

I stand up. I start feeling a little *roja*, but I speak anyway.

"I'm Stella. I'm nine. Well, nine and a third." I can tell I am speaking fast, so I try to slow down.

"I love the ocean. I just saw it in person for the first time in Mexico. I want to be a marine biologist and help protect the ocean. The ocean is my favorite place in the world."

"That's great. We'll teach you some ways you can help," says Mr. Kyle.

I feel my heart beating. I want to say so much more, but I am afraid, so I sit down.

"Who wants to go next?"

I'm a little frustrated. In my head, I had planned to go into a long speech where people would applaud, but I could only get those few words out. How can I be a crusader if I can't spread the word?

Then Kristen leans over.

"I want to save the oceans, too."

I look at her. She's not joking.

"Do you want to help me?" I ask.

She nods her head.

We stop talking because we get a few hushing looks from Ms. Susan. So we settle it by shaking pinkies.

I notice a few other kids as they present. Mariel talks about how she loves to go snorkeling.

"We used to go snorkeling when we were in Florida." She adds, "I want to be a zoologist."

I look over at her as she sits down. I try to smile at Mariel, but she doesn't notice. I hope I can turn things around with her. I've never met anyone who went snorkeling before.

Another kid, Logan, introduces himself as "obsessed with sharks." He says, "The megalodon is so cool! Too bad it's extinct." Logan has a Chicago accent. He's a little bit shorter than me, but my same age.

Another girl, Erika, shares with us that she's been whale watching. Then another boy, Dan, says, "I also want to be a marine biologist."

After everyone introduces themselves, Mr. Kyle and Ms. Susan stand up.

"Obviously everyone is here because they love the oceans. And I heard a few of you say you'd like to be a marine biologist."

A few kids and I nod at each other.

"Do you know what that means?"

Logan raises his hand.

"It's someone who studies the oceans."

"That's right," replies Ms. Susan.

"And there is a big range in what they do," says Mr. Kyle. "A marine biologist can study animals and their behaviors, microorganisms, how people affect the oceans, and how to protect the ocean's ecosystems. Just to name a few."

"Our job this week is to give you a sneak peek into all these categories. Our hope, for all of you, is that you'll leave here understanding the oceans and appreciate why they're so important to the planet," says Ms. Susan.

"And, of course, that you'll have fun, too. We'll give you firsthand experiences and have you all create projects with your own hands. For example, one year we had campers do experiments to learn about how blubber, feathers, and fur keep animals warm in cold ocean waters. Then they used what they learned to design a suit for themselves to keep warm in the wintertime."

The group murmurs with excitement.

Kristen whispers, "I want to do that."

"We'll discuss more about all of our projects later, but let's get started with a tour," says Mr. Kyle.

Then Mr. Kyle and Ms. Susan take us behind special locked doors. They have to wave their badges and type in a passcode to get in. Once the door buzzes open, they say, "It's magic time."

And we begin the tour.

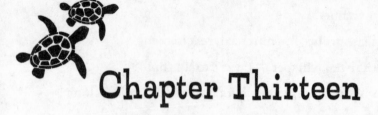

Chapter Thirteen

Mom picks me up at the end of the first day. She looks overwhelmed and is carrying a large leather bag with her.

"How did the *primer día* go?" she asks, taking off her high heels. She replaces them with ballet flats.

"AMAZING. I went on a behind-the-scenes, ultra-exclusive tour! The back area looks so scientific with pipes and computers. It looks like a submarine. I also think I may have one new friend who also wants to save the oceans."

Mom gives me a high five.

"See? The star worked." She smiles.

"What's in the leather bag?" I ask.

Mom softly moans. "I have to do work from home. That's how I can pick you up early every day this week."

When we get back home, I immediately call Jenny. I want to tell her about my first day of camp and see if she wants to help me save the oceans.

"Jenny, I'm on a mission. Meet me at the library."

"On my way," she replies.

I jump on my bike and ride to the library. When I see Jenny, I give her a big hug and hand her her gift. It's a colorful bag from Mexico that I filled with Japanese peanuts. For at least five minutes, I ramble about my trip. I haven't been able to tell her much since she was busy at dance camp.

"And I ate grasshoppers!" I conclude.

Jenny just shrugs.

"I ate duck eggs today," she replies. Her mom likes to buy pickled duck eggs from the Vietnamese market.

We both laugh. Even though it was just a few days, I missed Jenny. It's so great to have a best friend who understands that sometimes the food that doesn't sound familiar is actually the best.

She then tells me all about her camp and does a dance demonstration. I try my best to seem interested, but I really just want to get started on saving the oceans.

As soon as she finishes, I tell her our mission.

"In Mexico, I decided I'm going to be a marine biologist and protect the oceans! And I need your help."

"How are you going to protect them?" she asks.

I pause. That's a good question.

"All right, so I haven't figured out all the details. I just know the sea creatures need our help, and I thought we could do some research and figure out how to help them."

Jenny looks a little more convinced.

"I'll help when I'm not at dance camp or rehearsing. I have to practice a lot for my duet at the recital. That's coming up soon."

My stomach sinks a little. The oceans are more important than dancing. I wish Jenny understood that. I can't complain, though. A little help is better than nothing.

"Where do we start?" She stands on her tippy toes like a ballerina.

We begin by consulting our faithful friend, the library catalog. It's easy to find some books on the ocean on the computer, and we skim through the section a little bit. It's mostly books that I've seen before. As you can imagine, I know that area quite well.

Jenny says, "This is great stuff about oceans, but we need some tips on how to save them."

As much as I'd like to disagree, Jenny is right.

"Let's ask a librarian," I say as I stand up.

We find a librarian at the information desk. Jenny rings the bell to get his attention. It startles him for a second.

"How can I help you, young ladies?"

I speak up, pretending to be confident.

"I'm Stella, and this is my friend Jenny, and we'd

like to save the oceans. And we need help finding research."

"What go-getters! Follow me this way!"

He takes us over to the computers in the kids' section.

"I'd recommend searching for oceans, but also conservation."

"Of course, we learned about conservation last year!" I reply enthusiastically.

"Reduce, reuse, and recycle," adds Jenny.

I nod. I learned about it in Ms. Bell's class. The three R's are all about conservation. Conservation is about preserving and protecting natural resources. Recycling is making sure reusable materials are not thrown in the trash. Instead the materials can be recycled and turned into something new!

"But what does that have to do with the oceans?" I ask.

"Sadly," replies the librarian, "a lot of the trash we create ends up there."

"Oh . . . ," we reply. I never realized that before. I was so focused on protecting sea creatures from people—like building a fence around turtle nests—that I didn't realize we're hurting them from far away, too. Like polluting their homes with our trash.

The librarian finds us a list of books in the catalog that matches both conservation and oceans. With our arms full of books, we leave the library. It's more than enough to begin. At the last minute, Jenny grabs a book on baking for kids.

"It just looks too tasty," she says.

Back at home, we start on posters. Jenny writes out in bubble letters SAVE THE OCEANS while I draw a mighty blue whale underneath. It's the largest mammal, or animal, to have ever existed on the entire planet. It's a symbol worthy of the cause.

Then I start writing facts on a separate poster. Like how there are one hundred fifty million metric tons of plastic in all the oceans. If an elephant weighs a ton, then that's like one hundred fifty million elephants of trash! The more I write and read, the worse I feel about what we're doing to the oceans. I think learning about conservation might go hand in hand with feeling a little bad.

After we finish making the posters, I feel less upset, but like usual I want to do more. I lie down on my thinking rug.

"All the facts are sad, Jenny," I say, frowning. "I really hope I can figure out how to fix the oceans."

"A snack might make us smarter," Jenny says, looking at the baking book. She's been flipping through the pages as I worked on the posters.

We head to the kitchen and brainstorm over some *galletas* from the pantry. I don't know if it really made us feel smarter, but the cookies sure improved our spirits.

Chapter Fourteen

The second day of camp, Mr. Kyle and Ms. Susan introduce us to one of our big projects. At first, the project is sort of a mystery.

"It's best if we explain it in the penguin habitat," says Ms. Susan.

We all squeal together as a group.

In the habitat, we are not allowed to pet the penguins. It's still great, though. This is the closest I've ever been to a penguin. I'm within arm's length of cuddling one.

Kristen leans into me. "It smells sort of fishy in here."

I nod, but I really don't mind. Their little waddles and personalities are so funny. I can ignore the smell.

Mr. Kyle holds up a rubber ball and throws it at the penguins. They have so much fun pushing it around to each other. Almost like Biscuit with his toys.

"Today you're going to make toys for the animals. Similar to the ball I just threw. They're called enrichment toys. The toys help the animals exercise their minds and bodies."

"Awesome," replies Mariel. "If I'm not a zoologist, I definitely want to be a designer."

I try to smile at her. I'm determined to make her my friend, but she turns her head again before she can see me.

"Follow us. It's inspiration time," says Ms. Susan.

They take us to the official enrichment room. It's where they store all the toys that belugas, otters, sea lions, and dolphins play with. The toys come in all varieties. There are Frisbees, balls, Hula-Hoops, and even ice cubes in a cooler. I pick up a plastic figure. It sort of looks like a skeleton.

"That's the sea lion's favorite toy at Halloween," says Ms. Susan, grinning.

After we examine the enrichment toys, Mr. Kyle says, "As you design, imagine how the animals might engage their senses with the toy. Think about how the animals could play with your toy in their groups."

We get to work in the big craft room. The craft room is like our own personal art-supply store. It has all the supplies you can imagine.

"Now, before you get to work," says Ms. Susan, "we'd like for you to get into groups of threes."

Kristen and I naturally team up. We even ate lunch together yesterday. When we look around, it seems as if everyone has formed their groups. Everyone except for Mariel.

"Mariel, do you want to be part of our group?" asks Kristen.

Mariel shrugs her shoulders. The three of us sit

down at a table. We are a little silent as we sketch our ideas. I keep biting my lip trying to figure out what to say to Mariel. The thing is, I don't know where to begin. I know that she's been to Florida, but I've never been there so I don't know what to ask her about it. I've also never been snorkeling, so I can't talk about that. I even think about using a "conversation starter." Thankfully, Logan breaks the silence by asking Mr. Kyle a question.

"How did the animals end up here? Wouldn't they rather be in the oceans?"

Mr. Kyle sighs.

"You're right, but many of these animals are rescues. They were injured from fishing nets or tied up in plastic. The aquarium is a sanctuary for them, a safe place that is not quite their home but at least protects them from harm. Since their habitats here are smaller than their natural surroundings, they aren't able to do everything they would do regularly. For example, hunt for their own food or explore. Because of that the animals can get a little restless or bored. By making these toys for them, you're improving their quality of life."

I frown a little. I still love the aquarium because I can see the animals firsthand, but at the same time I feel sad for the animals. They are living far away from where they were born. I know how bad it feels when you feel like you don't belong. I want to make the oceans safe for all the sea creatures so they never have to leave. Unfortunately, this plastic problem is huge! I need to figure out a way to fix this.

Chapter Fifteen

When I get back home from camp, I
immediately call Jenny. I want to see if she wants
to help make more posters.

Her mom answers instead.

"Hi, Stella. Jenny is busy. She is rehearsing for her
recital."

I frown.

"Oh, okay," I reply. "Can you tell her I called?"

It's a little upsetting. I know Jenny cares less about
saving the oceans than I do. She spent most of our last
session reading the baking book from the library. It
made me a little mad. But she's also busy, and it's okay
if we have differences. At least that's what I tell myself.

Part of being a crusader is being flexible to obstacles. I have to be adaptable just like the tuna fish. Not only are they the only warm-blooded fish, they can raise their body temperature to adjust to colder water to stay warm.

Mom's busy working so I decide next to look for Nick in his room for help. Unfortunately, it's empty. Then I remember he is at the pizza shop. He's working extra all week because I'm at camp.

With no one to help me, I decide to read more about how we are polluting the oceans. The information is sad again. For instance, I read that sea turtles often confuse plastic bags with sea jellies, which they like to eat, so they end up eating the plastic bags by accident. I picture the baby sea turtles I just saw at the beach in Mexico. My heart breaks. Poor little guys.

The worst part is I read that even if everyone recycles, we're still using more and more plastic, much more than we can recycle. Plastic is even showing up on islands in the middle of the Pacific Ocean where people don't even live. And the animals there are suffering from it.

While I read this depressing information, Linda comes over. Mom promised her dinner since she took care of Pancho during our trip to Mexico. Linda sits in her favorite chair and knits as Mom cooks. She watches me push my books aside and curl up into a ball.

"Well, I've never seen you react to a book like this!" she exclaims. "Only my grandson, Joey, reacts like this. But he doesn't like to read. *Yet*."

Part of me wants to smile, but I can't.

"What's the matter, Stella?"

"It's the oceans. They're *dying*." I flop over dramatically onto my back.

"Oh . . . ," she says, dropping her knitting needles, ". . . it is really sad, isn't it?"

I look up at her face. She looks sincere. Biscuit runs onto the top of my stomach. He sits down and nuzzles his face against mine. It's almost as if he knew I needed a friend.

Linda slowly gets off the chair and sits closer to me.

"But you know what is amazing?"

I shake my head no.

"Is that you care so much."

I shrug.

"I know that doesn't sound helpful right now, but I know you're going to make a difference. And if you can get more people to help, you'll make a bigger change."

I sit up on my elbows. She has a point.

"Why don't you write Stanley an email? I'm sure your mom won't mind just one more. And after, maybe you can make a whole list of questions to ask your camp counselors tomorrow."

I sit all the way up. Biscuit barks almost as if he is motivating me.

I get Mom to turn on the computer. Linda knits nearby as I write an email to Stanley.

Dear Stanley,

I'm super bummed. Saving the oceans
is hard! It turns out there is so much
plastic and it's only getting worse.
I don't know what to do. I have made

some posters. Jenny helped some,
but she's so busy with dance camp
that I'm sort of on my own.

Your sad friend,
Stella

I draw a sad drawing of me in my sketchbook. I put teardrops all around me and some dead fish at my feet. After looking at it, I decide not to ask Mom to help me send the drawing with the email. That would be too dramatic. Instead, I only put a few sad emojis at the end.

After sending, I start making a list of things to ask my camp counselors. They've got to be able to help me. My biggest question is: How do we stop using so much plastic?

Chapter Sixteen

The next day at camp I walk in through the front doors, determined. Before Mr. Kyle and Ms. Susan start going over the schedule, I corner them.

"I've been reading . . . ," I begin.

"That's terrific. What about?" asks Ms. Susan.

"I read about how the oceans are filling up with plastic. I spent all afternoon being blue yesterday, but today, more than ever, I want to fix it."

I curl my fist and pump it.

Mr. Kyle and Ms. Susan look at each other and then nod at me.

"Awesome, young lady."

"But I don't know how," I reply, looking down at the ground.

"Hey, there. Don't worry. We'll give you some ideas. Promise," says Ms. Susan.

Once all the campers have arrived and settled down, Mr. Kyle speaks.

"Today we're going to work more on the enrichment toys, but I want to start the day talking about something else. I know many people are concerned about the oceans. Stella just came to us this morning feeling pretty blue about it."

I turn a little *roja*. I didn't know I'd be put on the spot.

"How many of you feel that way, too?"

Everyone else raises their hands. The *roja* fades away. I'm not alone.

"So I thought we could spend some time brainstorming ideas. Little things that we can do to make a change." Mr. Kyle continues, "Specifically, let's think of ways we can cut down on plastic."

I perk up. I'm all ears.

Mr. Kyle writes on the blackboard WAYS TO CUT DOWN ON PLASTIC.

"So do any of you have any ideas?"

Logan raises his hand. "You can carry a reusable bottle. My dad got me this one." He raises up his bottle. "It has sharks on it."

"That's a great idea. And remember you don't have to put just water in it. You can put in juice or coffee when you're older," responds Ms. Susan.

"Anyone else?" asks Mr. Kyle.

Kristen raises her hand.

"What about plastic straws? My mom said we shouldn't use them anymore."

I gulp. I love plastic straws.

"That's a great idea," replies Mr. Kyle, writing it down. "And there are some great reusable straws, too, made out of silicone and stainless steel."

Whew. I feel relieved. Then I think of one.

"Could people use tote bags instead of plastic bags? My neighbor Linda always carries one around."

"Yes! And make sure to say no to one when you're offered a plastic bag," says Mr. Kyle, writing my suggestion on the board next to the other two ideas.

"Does anyone else have an idea?" says Ms. Susan.

The room grows silent. Everyone is scratching their heads trying to come up with an idea.

Ms. Susan raises her hand. "Can I suggest one?"

We all nod our heads.

"What about plastic spoons, forks, and knives? Just bring your own with you and say no when someone like a restaurant offers you some."

"Fabulous," says Mr. Kyle, writing it down.

Ms. Susan says, "This is a great start and these are only four recommendations. But if all of you follow them, then it can make a big impact. And if you all spread the word, it can have an even bigger effect."

I look at the list on the board.

This is easy! I can do this, I think.

Then Mr. Kyle says, "And one last suggestion. There is a great article called 'Planet or Plastic' in *National Geographic.*"

Kristen raises her hand. "I know that article. I stopped reading it. It was too sad."

"I completely agree. It's heartbreaking, but its sole purpose is to inform. You know, sometimes you have to confront people with really hard information to make them realize how important the cause is," says Mr. Kyle.

I nod. It's so upsetting. But now that I know more about how we're harming the oceans, I have to save them, and I'm going to tell everyone about the plastic crisis. At least try. Even if it's scary to talk to new people. This is too important.

"But the best part of the article is that at the end there is a pledge. By signing the pledge, you agree to stop using so much plastic, because you love the oceans more."

"I can do that." I'm so determined that I speak aloud without thinking.

"I thought so," replies Ms. Susan. "Especially coming from the future Sylvia Earle."

1. Carry a Reusable Bottle

2. Say No to Plastic Straws

3. Carry a Tote Bag and Say no to Plastic Bags

4. Say No to Plastic Cutlery

Chapter Seventeen

When Mom picks me up from camp today, she's distracted. She ends up talking on her cell phone with people from work on the ride home on the Metra. I'm not able to tell her my latest developments from camp yet.

At home, we are greeted by another ringing phone. This time it's the house phone. "Stella, it's for you!" says Mom.

I pick up the phone expecting that it's Dad. I sent him a present from Mexico.

"*Hola*, Stella. It's me, Stanley."

I gasp. This is the best surprise.

"I got your email. My dad said it sounded like you

needed a real phone call. Are you still sad about the oceans?"

I'm far from sad now that I have some ideas from camp. But I'm lucky to have a friend who cares.

"I'm doing much better," I say. "My camp counselors gave me some information on how to cut down on plastic."

"Tell me so I can start telling everyone."

I read out loud the four recommendations and tell him how he could sign the *National Geographic* pledge online.

"Easy peasy! Hey, what if you make your own pledge from the points? If everyone signs it, we'd save a lot of plastic from going into the oceans."

I gasp. That is a good idea!

Stanley also thanks me for my postcard and letter. He says he was jealous that I had such a cool adventure in Mexico.

"How was the rest of Space Camp?" I ask.

"Awesome! I met a real-life astronaut. His name is Leland Melvin. He was in the NFL until he got injured and then became an astronaut with hard work."

"Wow!" I reply.

Then he says, "Yeah, he's my new hero, but I'll be back next week, and I can tell you more about it then. I'll be happy to help you save the oceans, too."

"Deal," I reply.

After hanging up, I check in with Mom. I'm positive she'll be happy to sign my new pledge.

Mom is working on her laptop in her bedroom. She looks a little busy, but this is important.

"We need to stop using so much plastic," I say from the doorway.

Mom looks deep in thought at her computer.

"Mmmmm."

"*Mom* . . . ," I reply.

Mom closes her laptop a little. "*Mi amor*, give me one hour of work time, and I'll be all ears. I promise."

I spend the next hour going around the house, pulling out plastic bags and plastic bottles. I start with our kitchen pantry then move to the bathrooms and the trash bins. I pile all of them onto the kitchen counter. Like Ms. Susan said, sometimes you need to confront people with the hard facts.

Finally, Mom comes out of her bedroom.

"Stella . . . ," she says, sounding a little annoyed. I can tell because her voice gets much deeper. Her eyes are fixed on the plastic collection.

"¿Qué haces?"

"I'm trying to find all the plastic in the house to demonstrate how much we use."

Mom touches her head in frustration.

"I see," she says, holding her hands on her hips. "Well, it's very messy in here."

Oh no, I think. My demonstration is not Mom-approved. If there is one thing Mom doesn't care for it's messes. But I just wanted to show her why this is important. I have to fix this.

"I'll clean it up, but see—we use a lot of plastic! So much."

Mom doesn't quite look convinced.

"It takes almost five hundred years for a plastic bottle to decompose," I say, holding a bottle of water. Then I grab my journal.

"Look! I have this to read! And I wrote down this list from camp today. I'm going to turn it into a pledge that everyone can sign."

She grabs my journal and takes one long deep breath.

"You read this on the couch and I'll put everything away," I say, trying to smile extra big.

Mom moves to the living room and begins to read while I put everything back in its proper place. When everything is organized, I join Mom on the couch. She looks more relaxed, but is still more serious than usual.

"I know this is important to you," Mom replies.

Her voice sounds controlled like she's being deliberate with every word. "And I will sign the pledge and promise to cut back on plastic."

I exhale a big sigh of relief. Not only is Mom no longer upset, she's going to sign the pledge!

Then Mom adds, "But you also have to be okay that we might use some plastic in the future. Can you promise me that?"

"I promise," I reply. I feel better knowing Mom is not really mad. Even better, we're going to cut down on plastic as well.

"I also had a thought while you were cleaning up," she says, pointing to my list.

"If we're going to stop using plastic bags, we're going to need more tote bags."

I nod. That's true.

"And we have all this leftover fabric in our craft box. Why don't we try making our own tote bags?"

I squeal. That's the best idea.

"Can we do that tonight after dinner?" I ask.

"*Sí*," she replies.

Later that night, Mom and I use the sewing machine to make tote bags. We add leftover crazy fabric to make them as eccentric as possible.

"Who says being green has to be *aburrido*!" Mom says, holding a zigzag fabric.

As always, Mom is right. Going green isn't boring.

Chapter Eighteen

On the fourth day of camp, Ms. Susan and Mr. Kyle spend some more time talking about ocean conservation.

"We've had requests for more information. We also thought it was time to share some happier news," says Ms. Susan.

I find out that many places are making big strides with plastic. For instance, some cities like San Francisco have even banned plastic bags. Many businesses are eliminating plastic straws. Some countries like Denmark are so green friendly that a person there only uses on average four plastic bags a year.

I raise my hand. I'm feeling nervous, but I want to

share my new pledge with the group. I spent an hour this morning designing it with fun bubble letters. Even Mom agreed it looked great. I'm a little scared to ask everyone separately to sign so I decide to start with Mr. Kyle first. He is easier to talk to, and he has a louder voice than I do anyway.

"I was thinking about our four points yesterday that we wrote down, and I made it into a pledge. I am thinking maybe everyone could sign it?"

"That's brilliant," says Mr. Kyle. "Will everyone sign Stella's pledge?"

I look around timidly. To my surprise, everyone is nodding their head.

"Why don't you pass it around?" adds Ms. Susan.

I pass it to Kristen who passes it to Logan. One by one, all the campers sign the pledge. I even get a few thumbs-up. Finally, Kristen brings the pledge back to me.

"This is so smart. I also love how you drew the letters," says Kristen.

"It just doesn't feel like enough," I reply. "I want

more people to sign. It feels like there is only so much I can do, and this is a gigantic problem."

"I feel the same way," she replies.

Suddenly Kristen jumps up. "I've got it. Maybe we should start a group, that way we can do more together."

"That's a great idea!" I reply.

Then I pause. "But I don't know how to do that. Do you?"

I raise my eyebrows at her.

"Me either," says Kristen, "but there is no harm in trying."

Before we can chat about it more, we move on to finishing our enrichment toys. I'm pleased with the design Kristen, Mariel, and I came up with. We took a Hula-Hoop and attached different shapes out of rubber and strips

of fabric. We designed our toy with dolphins in mind. Dolphins are one of the smartest mammals and love to play. We hope that it will keep them entertained. I realize, though, as I hold the toy in my hands, how little I spoke to Mariel during our group project. I just could never figure out what to say to her. She always looked like she was deep in thought . . . or worse. Like maybe she doesn't like me. How am I going to start a group if I can't speak to everyone?!

At lunchtime, I begin to talk to Kristen more about the club idea when out of the blue Logan joins our table. I haven't spoken to him much, but he seems nice and excited about things he really likes.

"Kristen told me that you have a save-the-oceans group," he says.

I sit back. Kristen looks sheepish.

I am surprised, but I feel happy. I guess Kristen decided to start the club idea for us.

"We've just started," I reply. "It's just a couple of us."

Logan looks disappointed. Oh no, I'm underselling this.

I enthusiastically reply, "But we have ideas. I've made posters with my best friend, Jenny."

Logan stares at me, waiting for me to say more. This happens often when I'm feeling shy. Then I remember Jenny's baking book and have a moment of inspiration.

"And we're going to do a bake sale and give all the money to an ocean charity."

"We are?" says Kristen. She looks excited.

I shrug and nod.

Logan replies, "That's great, but we've got to do more."

"I think so, too. Do you have any suggestions?" I ask.

Logan grabs his chin.

"And maybe we can get people to sign the pledge you mentioned, at the bake sale," he replies.

My mouth drops. That's even better.

"I like that! We could make a printout, and

everyone could take it home with them to help remind them," Kristen exclaims.

Logan shakes his head. "That will waste paper."

I frown. He's right. If we're going to be green, we
need to be not wasteful.

"What if we make a blog page?" responds Kristen.
"My older sister has one and she could help us get
one up."

"That's a good idea," replies Logan.

Mr. Kyle comes over. "I couldn't help but overhear.
I know it's not the ocean, but we have something you
can do right here. We have a cleanup day at the beach

at Lake Michigan. It's this Saturday. Ms. Susan and I will be there."

"Yes!" we all shout.

Mr. Kyle leaves, and I pull out my notebook so that Kristen and Logan can write down their phone numbers. As I look at their handwriting, I feel encouraged. I have an official group! Perhaps together we can really help make a big change. At least it will be more than I could have done all alone.

Chapter Nineteen

After camp, I tell Mom about the beach cleanup day on our Metra ride. She's pumped.

"*¡Qué padre!* It's great that we're starting in our own backyard. Count me in!"

"And some of the kids from camp are going to be there, too," I reply.

"I can't wait." She smiles.

The happy mood changes quickly when we get back home. Mom receives an email saying that they need her help at work this Saturday. Unfortunately, this means she's going to have to work during the beach cleanup.

"Don't worry, *mi amor*. I'll ask your brother."

For the first time all week, Nick is home in the afternoon and not at the pizza shop. It's hard to tell, though, because he is hiding in his room.

Mom heads up to talk to him. I sneak up closer for a better listen. Right away, I can tell he is not enthusiastic about this.

"But, Mom, I was going to hang out with my friends on Saturday. Not my kid sister."

"*Lo siento, niño*, but I really could use your help with this. You know we've only got each other."

"What about Linda?"

"You know it's too far for Linda to have to go."

He groans.

Mom continues. "Plus, it's for a good cause. Why don't you invite Jason? That way you can hang out with your friend at the same time."

"All right. I guess. I'll ask him if he wants to go," replies Nick, letting out a big sigh.

"Thank you, *niño*. *Tú eres el mejor hijo*," she replies, saying he is the best son.

I walk back to the kitchen quietly before Mom sees me.

"He's going to take you," Mom says, returning with a big smile on her face.

"Great," I reply, but really, I feel a little bad. I don't know why Nick doesn't want to hang out with me. Maybe Nick has been replaced by his secret twin brother. And the twin is named Nicolas. And that twin doesn't like me as much. At least I hope so. That would be easier to accept than Nick not wanting to be around me anymore.

"Why don't you ask Jenny, too?" Mom suggests.

That's a good idea. I could use my best friend right now. Why didn't I think of her first?

But when I call Jenny, like Nick, she's not enthusiastic about it.

"I can't, Stella. I have to practice for my recital."

I groan. "You're always busy now."

"Dancing is important to me," says Jenny, sounding very annoyed.

"I know, *okay*. It's all you talk about," I reply. I

can't believe how selfish Jenny is being. The oceans are in crisis, especially the marine life. Now is not the time for dancing.

"Stella, you're not being a good best friend to me right now," replies Jenny.

Frustrated, I blurt out, "But this is more important than dancing!"

I cover my mouth. Even though I had been thinking it, it sounded really bad when I said it out loud.

Jenny is silent on the phone.

"I'm so sorry, Jenny. I don't mean that." My face turns *roja* with embarrassment.

"It's okay, Stella, but I should go now."

We say our goodbyes.

When I hang up, I feel awful. Jenny isn't being selfish, I am. As much as I want to save the oceans, I need to fix things with Jenny first.

I work on a poster-size "I'm sorry" card for Jenny until bedtime.

The next day is the last day of the Shedd summer camp. To celebrate, we finally share our enrichment toys with the animals. The dolphins squeak and whistle when we give them the toy we designed.

"I think that means they like it," says Mr. Kyle.

Mariel smiles proudly at me for a second.

I take this as my last opportunity to try to talk to Mariel. I have to at least try. I take a breath and say, "You did a really good job."

"Thanks. I'm sad camp is ending," Mariel replies.

"Me too."

I pause and decide to ask her to join the conservation group.

"It's a way for us to make a big difference. We can't do it alone. Plus, we will be able to still hang out. That way camp sort of doesn't have to end."

I tell her that we've just started and then she replies, "I overheard you guys at lunch."

It occurs to me that I haven't seen her sitting with anyone at lunch all week. Could it be that Mariel is a little shy, too? She doesn't seem like it. She looks calm in comparison to me when I'm nervous. I've never seen her turn *roja* or sweat.

"So do you want to join?"

She nods. I can't tell if she's excited or not, but it's a step in the right direction with her. I add, "We're going to talk about it more at the cleanup. Will you be there?"

She shrugs. "I have to check with my parents," she replies, "but I do want to come."

At the end of the day, I wave goodbye to my new friends. Mom throws her arm around my shoulders.

"By the look of it, I'd say it was a pretty successful week, Estrellita."

It really was, but I have something else to do right now.

"Mom, can we drop something off at Jenny's to-night?"

"Of course. Let's do it when we pick up *el niño* from work."

I sigh. I had a good day with my new friends, but nothing feels right until I get my best friend back. I hope my poster-size card works.

Chapter Twenty

Nick acts normal the day of the beach cleanup and doesn't mention anything to me about being forced to come. We ride the Metra with Jason to Lake Michigan. When we arrive, the beach is filled with strangers, young and old, ready to help. I never knew so many people cared.

"Whoa . . . it's busy," says Jason.

At the beach, I get excited when I see Kristen, Logan, Ms. Susan, and Mr. Kyle. Then I spy Mariel. I am glad she came, but it definitely means I'm going to have to try harder today to win her over.

"Welcome, everyone," says Mr. Kyle with a bullhorn.

"Thank you for coming to our beach cleanup. We do this a few times a year."

"And we post the dates online," says Ms. Susan, leaning over to speak into Mr. Kyle's horn.

Mr. Kyle pauses and resumes speaking.

"While Lake Michigan isn't an ocean, this lake is just as important to us. Not only is it a majestic body of water to look at but this lake is also home to over three thousand plant and animal species, not to mention forty million people. This water right next to us eventually ends up in our beloved oceans through the rivers and streams. If we want to keep our oceans clean, we've got to start right at home."

I gasp. It's amazing how all the water on earth is connected. Each body of water affects the other.

"Now, I have thick gloves, paper bags, and sticks for everyone to pick up the litter. So if you're ready, come on up!"

As we pick up the trash, Nick goes off with Jason, leaving me with my new club members.

The majority of what we find is just plastic

bottles, cans, and food wrappers. Occasionally we find something weird like a stuffed toy or T-shirt. A toy I understand. Kids leave toys behind all the time. They must have been sad, but who loses a T-shirt?

While we pick up the random trash, Logan brings up what he'd like to do with the club.

"I want to raise so much money just like my cousin Mary. She raised money to save the sea otters all by herself!"

Although I'm impressed by Logan's cousin, I have a hard time listening to him. That's because I notice Nick talking to a couple of older girls with Jason. He points over at me and rolls his eyes. I overhear him say, "I'm here because of my annoying little sister. She always drags me to stuff like this."

It hurts more than a bee sting. The way he's saying it makes it seem like I'm just a pest. Thankfully, Mariel starts talking.

"I've been thinking. What's the name of the club?"

I look down. I can't believe I hadn't considered a name. That's, like, step one of forming a club.

"Every club has a good name," she says.

I turn a little *roja*. I hope that everyone doesn't think I'm not prepared enough, especially Mariel.

"The Ocean Crusaders?" I suggest.

Mariel shrugs. "That's not catchy enough."

I look from side to side frantically. I cover my mouth with my hand and take a secret deep breath. With a clear head, I've got it! I remember that Jacques Cousteau started a group with his friends Philippe and Frédéric called the Sea Musketeers. Maybe that could be the name of our group!

I blurt out, "The Sea Musketeers."

"I like it!" says Kristen, flashing her braces at me.

Logan nods. "Well, I think it's a contender. We should vote at our first meeting."

"When is that going to be?" asks Mariel.

I gulp. I hadn't planned that far.

Quickly I reply, "Let's have our first meeting next weekend at my place. I'll have to check with my mom first, but I think it should be okay."

We collect trash the rest of the morning. Mr. Kyle said it was the largest group they have ever had on a beach cleanup day. It's awesome to know that we did something big together.

After we're done volunteering and Jason goes home, I walk alone with Nick. I feel exhausted from being in the sun all morning long, and now that it's the afternoon, it's only getting hotter. I really could go for ice cream, but I don't feel like suggesting fun things to do with Nick right now. Especially after what he said about me.

"Why are you so quiet?" he says, messing with my curls.

"No reason," I reply, not looking at him.

I didn't have the words to tell him. He has never made fun of me in front of other people before. It hurts even more because I think my big brother is pretty awesome, most of the time.

He shrugs. "I had a great time. I met a girl who is going to be in my high school next year."

He looks a little lovesick.

"But I thought you said girls were gross."

"Just you," he replies.

I cross my arms. We walk the rest of the way home in silence.

Chapter Twenty-One

When we get back from the beach cleanup, I find Mom curled up on the couch covered with a knitted blanket. She's taking a nap after working at the office. I snuggle in with her. She sleepily asks, "How was the beach cleanup?"

"Good," I reply.

Then I fall silent.

"What's wrong?" she says, sitting up. "I thought you'd be speaking nonstop once you got home."

"Nick made fun of me, and it seems like he doesn't like to hang out with me anymore. And why does he want to be called Nicolas now? He's always been Nick.

And now he doesn't think girls are gross anymore. It's too much." The corners of my eyes well up with tears. I never realized how much it was bothering me until I said it out loud.

"Oh, you're being *mensa*, Stella. He does love you . . ." Then she stops. I can tell she's choosing her words carefully.

"He does, he really does. He's just getting older and wanting to sound grown-up. That's why he wants to be called Nicolas."

"Why does he make fun of me?" I ask. I can feel my lip quivering a little.

"It's complicated. Sometimes he says mean things, but he really doesn't mean it."

"I'm not sure about that. I don't like this 'Nicolas.'" I mush my face into Mom's shoulder.

"I swear. Did you know he ignored me at his birthday pizza party?"

I shake my head.

"I felt upset, but then I thought about it . . . I was a teenager once and I was *igual o peor*. He is tame next to me," she laughs.

I raise my eyebrows.

"Really?"

"But I'll tell you more about that later. You're a little young for that."

I am dumbfounded. I can't imagine Mom not being sweet. She's Miss Responsibility.

"As for the name thing, there might be a day when you will want to be called Estrella."

I shake my head.

"Never."

"You might, and I'll call you Estrella if that's what you want. But in my heart, I'll always be calling you *mi bebé*."

She pulls me into a hug. I normally would groan a little after her calling me a baby, but today I don't mind at all.

"And one day you might like someone, too," she whispers.

"I've got too many things to worry about now, *Mom*," I reply. "Right now, I'm like a captain. My only love is the sea."

"Okay," she replies with a sly smile. "Well, tell me one good thing. There has to be one thing from the beach cleanup, right?"

I grin. There is.

"Well, my ocean group has an official name, I think. We're the Sea Musketeers."

"Great."

"And we're up to five people including me," I add smugly.

"Increíble."

Mom stands up and stretches her arms overhead.

"And that's not all . . . Can we host a club meeting next weekend in our *casa*?"

She lowers her arms back down. She's speechless. I can tell she's a bit surprised, but also pleased.

"*Sí, sí. Claro que sí,*" she says quickly. Then she puts her hands to her face.

"Oh, I'll have to get little snacks for you guys. *Una fiesta.*" Mom cha-chas a little.

"This is work, Mom. Important work."

I cross my arms and give her a serious stare.

Mom smiles.

"Yes. I'll get only serious snacks like bagel bites."

"No balloons," I add. "That's unnecessary and adds more plastic to the oceans."

She gives me two thumbs-up. Then she says, "Oh, by the way, Jenny called. She said to call her back."

She must have gotten the card. I hope that means she accepts my apology and not that she wants to tell me that she no longer wants to be my best friend. My heart beats fast when I dial her number. When Jenny picks up the phone, I immediately say, "I'm really sorry, Jenny."

"I know. But I've also been thinking. I'm a little guilty, too. I think we both haven't been as supportive to each other as we could have been."

"I promise to be a better best friend," I reply.

"Me too. So how was the beach cleanup?"

"Good! We cleaned up a bunch of trash. Mr. Kyle said that the whole volunteer group picked up over a hundred pounds of trash. The most ever collected."

"Way to go!" Jenny says.

"My club also has an official name, too."

"Oh," Jenny replies. "I didn't know you had a club."

Jenny sounds a little sad, which makes me feel bad. I know what will make her feel better.

Quickly, I reply, "Yeah, we're going to save the oceans. We're starting with a bake sale. I got inspired by the book you checked out from the library."

"Really?" Jenny replies, sounding much happier.

"Yeah, I couldn't have done this without my best friend. If you're not too busy, you can come to our first meeting. It's at my house."

"Yes! I'd love to. Anything that involves baking and my best friend. I'm in."

I smile and reply, "Now tell me all about dance camp."

While Jenny talks about her upcoming recital, I feel relieved. I know that Jenny and I might have different interests, but as long as we take the time to listen to each other we will be A-OK.

Chapter Twenty-Two

In my almost nine and a half years of life, I have never had a big group of kids over. Except my birthday parties in kindergarten and first grade. In my book, those do not count. Back then, Mom always made me invite everyone in my class to come because it's polite. I even had to invite Jessica Anderson. She even avoided talking to me at my own party!

This time is different. I am over-the-moon excited about having my first big group hangout at home. Everyone who is coming over wants to come over. Nobody is being forced. The best part is that Stanley is going to be there, too! He just got back from Texas. I haven't seen him yet, but he called yesterday and promised to be there.

Mom had one requirement before allowing me to have everyone come over. She insisted everything in the house be sparkling clean for my club meeting.

"A clean house makes a person feel welcomed," she says.

I nod my head. I don't love cleaning, but if this is what I have to do to have my meeting in the house, I'll do it!

First thing Saturday morning, Mom reviews my tasks before my group comes over.

"Okay, Ms. Sea Musketeer. Will you clean your room and *el baño*?"

"Yes! I'll clean my room and the bathroom. I'll even clean under my bed," I reply.

As I clean, I find weird things under my bed like one of Biscuit's dog treats. I guess he has another favorite spot in our home besides our backyard.

By the time I'm done cleaning, Nick comes down for breakfast. He still has a blanket wrapped around him. He drapes himself with a blanket whenever he is sleepy.

"I could hear you two giggling earlier," says Nick, mumbling.

Nick slumps over on the couch. I'm still a little hurt when I think about the cleanup day. I've been sort of ignoring him. It's been easy since he's been at work, but then I think about what Mom said, and I decide to give it a try. I walk over to him.

"Nick, could you help me with my club?"

"What club?" he asks drowsily.

My feelings are a little hurt, but at least he's listening to me.

"My saving-the-oceans club. The kids from the beach cleanup, me, plus Stanley, and Jenny have started a club called the Sea Musketeers. We want to raise money to save the oceans."

I show him the pledge I designed. It has all the signatures from camp.

"This looks great," he says, handing it back to me.

"Our first meeting is today. Will you come?"

"Oh . . ." He rubs his eyes. "I'm going to hang out with my friends from work today. But I'll be an unofficial member, okay?"

I frown a little.

Nick notices that I'm let down.

"What if . . . I'm your club mentor. That's even better than a member. I can help you with ideas. All the best companies have a mentor."

I smile a little and shrug.

"I'll take that as a yes. Now pour me a glass of chocolate milk, and we'll get started."

Turns out Nick is a pretty great mentor. On the Marine Mammal Center website, he finds a way for the group to create its own fund-raising page. We decide that's who we are going to donate our bake sale money to. With Mom's permission, we create a page.

After breakfast, Nick goes back to his room. That's okay with me, too. Because soon there is a knock on the door. It's Stanley!

"Howdy, Stella! I'm here for our meeting."

His skin is tanned from all the time spent

outdoors in Texas. I give him a hug even though his hands are filled.

In one hand, he has a box of his M&M cookies.

"Mom and I thought that I might need them since I am meeting new kids." He grins.

In the other, he is carrying a new book entitled *Fifty Ways to Save the Ocean*. On the back it has in big letters "Clean, Protect, Conserve—and Enjoy—Our Magnificent Oceans."

"That's for our meeting," he says. "I've been doing my own research, too. I also have a crowd-pleasing joke. Want to hear it?"

"Sure!"

Stanley leans in. "What did the Pacific Ocean say to the Atlantic Ocean?"

"I don't know," I reply.

Stanley starts giggling. "Nothing. It just *waved*."

I groan. The joke might not be the best, but it's great to have Stanley back.

Jenny shows up next. I give her a super tight hug.

"I made you another best-friend bracelet," she says.

As I place the bracelet next to the other on my wrist, I know everything is fine between us.

Before the rest of the group shows up, Jenny shows off her completed choreography to Stanley and me. Jenny's performance is marvelous!

"You're so good, Jenny!" I say.

She bows. When she lifts up her head, her face is glowing.

"Thank you. We're going to have our recital next week. Will you come? They're going to have a big reception and everything."

"Yes . . ." Suddenly, I have a bright idea. The biggest and greatest idea.

"Guys, what if we do our bake sale there?"

"At the dance recital?" asks Jenny.

Stanley high-fives me.

Jenny squeals. "Yes! I mean I think we have to check, but there will be plenty of people."

The doorbell starts ringing. One by one, everyone shows up. Mariel is the last to arrive. I open the door to almost everyone except for Mariel. I was too busy grabbing the snacks for the group. I didn't even realize she made it until I headed over to the living room to check. I glance over to see Mariel speaking Spanish with Mom perfectly. Mariel even makes Mom laugh!

"I like her. She has such a fun Puerto Rican accent," Mom whispers to me when I enter the living room.

I feel a little *roja*, but this time, it's jealousy. I envy that Mariel can speak Spanish so well with my mom. She can even tell her jokes that make her laugh. The only time Mom laughs when I speak in Spanish is when I've made a "cute" mistake. Then I realize maybe if I had tried to speak some Spanish with Mariel I might have learned more about her. Like I never knew Mariel was Puerto Rican, and I was with her all week. I just never bothered to ask her questions like *Where are you from?* or *What is your favorite color?* I was just too intimidated and concerned about myself to try.

Mariel is inspecting our home. She picks up my

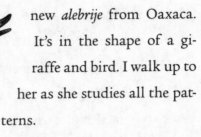

new *alebrije* from Oaxaca. It's in the shape of a giraffe and bird. I walk up to her as she studies all the patterns.

"Hi. The meeting is up in my room."

"What's this? I like it," asks Mariel as she touches the wings.

"It's an *alebrije*. It's from Mexico. It's a fantastical creature that is supposed to be a guide for people in the afterlife."

"That's cool!" She smiles, putting it down.

"My mom says you're from Puerto Rico?" I ask.

"Yup, well my family is. My parents moved to Miami before they had me. I was born there."

"Cool."

Then there is a long pause. I'm not sure what else to ask her right now, and the club is waiting.

"Well, let's go to the meeting," I reply.

Mariel follows me up to my room, and we launch our first meeting.

Logan begins by asking everyone if they agree on the name Sea Musketeers for the group. We get five yeses and one gigantic "Awesome" from Stanley.

"Now that that's settled," I continue, "we might have the perfect location for our bake sale. Jenny's dance recital."

"It's one of the largest dance camps in the city, and many people will be there, too," adds Jenny proudly.

"Great idea!" says Kristen.

"Should we have anything else at the bake sale besides the pledge?" asks Stanley. I see that he has no problem fitting in. Like usual, he just handed out his M&M cookies. As I pick up a cookie, I begin to feel a little nervous. I don't have anything else to add. I'm out of new ideas for my group already. I regret hosting the club at my *casa*. I can't sneak away from my own house.

"That reminds me," says Kristen. "My sister started a blog page with the pledge."

Suddenly, I have something to add.

"Wait, I have a fund-raising page, too. My brother, Nick, helped me set it up," I reply. I exhale. I guess I do have more to offer the group.

"Perfect, let's look at them both," says Logan. I feel relieved.

Mom brings up the laptop so we can look at the pages. Everyone gives feedback, everyone except for Mariel. She's too busy studying my new tote bag hanging on my door.

"Where did you get that?" asks Mariel.

"That's a tote bag Stella and I made," Mom replies proudly. "We're going to start using them instead of plastic bags."

"They're very artistic. What if we sell them at the bake sale? We could sell them for more money than a cookie," says Mariel.

We gasp. That's a good suggestion.

"Yes!" we all say together.

"We'll raise so much money," I reply. My eyes are filled with dollar signs.

"Thousands," chimes in Logan.

"Millions," adds Kristen.

"I doubt millions," says Mariel skeptically.

"Regardless of the amount, it's definitely a start," says Stanley.

Mariel stands up. "We definitely should have at least one other meeting. We need to make all the posters, plan the decorations, and figure out who is going to make what. Let's do my place next time. My parents already said it's fine."

I'm a little annoyed that Mariel is taking over the meeting some, but she has a point. I am very curious to know where she lives. I might even get more clues to who Mariel is, because right now she's a bit of a mystery.

Chapter Twenty-Three

Once we have the approval from Jenny's dance teacher to hold our bake sale at their recital, the Sea Musketeers go to work. Each person in the group is responsible for bringing at least one item for the bake sale. Jenny's already decided on Vietnamese donuts, and Stanley's bringing limeade. Stanley says you can't find good limeade outside of Texas and that his limeade "is going to blow everyone's minds."

Even Linda signs on to help. She's inspired by our tote bags and agrees to make a few, but out of yarn. While Mom and I plan on making more tote bags, Mom has the idea to include a free instructional guide at the bake sale on how to make an easy tote bag. That way if people don't want to buy a bag, they can still learn to make their own.

I even ask Dad for money when he finally calls to thank me for his present from Mexico. After I tell him about the tasty *chapulines*, I tell him about my crusade. I ask Dad to stop using plastic straws and bags.

He responds, "I'll try."

I'm a little skeptical, but he could surprise me.

When I go to the next Sea Musketeer's meeting, I discover that Mariel lives not that far from me. She only lives a little bit closer to downtown Chicago than I do. Since our meeting is on a Saturday, Mom drops me off.

I can hear *salsa* music from the front door of Mariel's house. I knock cautiously. My first knock is too soft so Mom has to knock again.

An old woman answers the door. She's wearing a giant shawl around her shoulders.

"*¿Quién es?*"

"I'm Stella." The old woman doesn't respond.

"*Me llamo Stella*," I repeat, this time in Spanish. She looks confused.

Mom steps in.

"*Buenos días, señora. Estamos buscando a Mariel.*"

"*Sí*," I say, agreeing that we're looking for a Mariel.

"Ahh, *sí, la amiga de Mariel. Mucho gusto.*"

The old woman says this in a way that's easy for me to follow. I'm sort of shocked, though, by what she says. Then she leans away from the door.

"*Mi amorcita? Es tu amiguita.*"

This old woman just called me Mariel's friend twice. She must be mistaken or not know Mariel too well because we're clearly not friends yet.

"*Un momento, abuelita.*" I hear Mariel saying that she'll only be a moment to her grandmother. This makes sense. The old woman reminds me of a friend-lier version of my own *abuela*.

"*Por favor, entra*," Mariel's grandmother says, wel-coming us inside.

Mom turns to me. "Do you want me to wait with you?"

"I'm okay. I understand her," I reply.

Mom kisses me on the top of the head and leaves. Mariel's grandmother tells me in Spanish to sit on the couch and that Mariel will be there soon.

While I wait, I study Mariel's house. It's brightly colored in oranges and pinks. It almost looks tropi-cal with all the wicker and plants. I even see a parrot the color of a mango in a cage.

Mariel enters the living room. "Good, you're on time."

I'm always on time, I think.

Instead I reply, "Is that your *abuela*?"

"Yeah, she moved in with us this year from Puerto Rico. She's getting older, and with the hurricanes, my parents decided she should move in with us."

"Wow," I reply.

Mariel nods. "It's nice to have her with us. We just moved to Chicago. She's like having a piece of home here."

"I didn't know you were new here," I reply.

"My dad got a new job, but I don't really like it here. I miss all my friends in Florida. I had a bunch of friends who I could speak Spanish with. I also miss the ocean."

Mariel slumps forward a little. Suddenly, I understand her a bit better. She wasn't upset with me that first day because I didn't speak Spanish. She was just disappointed that I wasn't exactly like one of her friends back in Miami. Maybe I should worry less about whether I fit in with other Latinos or not.

"Well, I don't speak Spanish perfectly, but I'll be your friend. Maybe you can help me get better at speaking *español*, too."

Mariel's eyes sparkle a little.

"I'd like that," she replies.

"My Mexico trip is the first time I ever swam in the ocean. And I already miss it. I understand why you miss it so much."

"Yeah, I could see all these tropical fishes, especially when we went to Key West."

"Amazing," I reply.

Before the rest of the kids show up, Mariel shows me some of the pictures she's taken of fishes underwater. I spy a blue tang and a banded butterfish. There is even a picture of a spiny lobster. Spiny lobsters are different from regular lobsters because they don't have claws. Instead they have two huge armor-plated

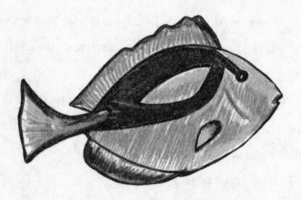

antennae. Her shark pictures probably scare me the most, but it does remind me of a "conversation starter" I wrote down.

"Did you know that sharks and dolphins are lighter on the bottom and darker on the top so they can camouflage themselves in the water?"

"I didn't know that. Tell me more," says Mariel.

Secretly, I squeal. That was one of the conversation starters I had planned to use at school, but this seems like the best time to really start a conversation.

"Well, when you're on top of the water looking down things look dark, but when you're swimming underwater, things look lighter because you're looking up at the sun."

"Wow, I never realized that. You're right!"

I smile. It feels nice to have finally started a real conversation with Mariel.

When the rest of the Sea Musketeers show up, we spend the afternoon making a giant banner and a list of everything we'll need.

"We'll need pens. I'll bring those," says Kristen.

"And I can bring plastic plates and cups," says Jenny.

"No." Logan shakes his head. "That just creates more plastic waste."

Jenny looks embarrassed. I quickly say, "It's okay. Could you bring some paper napkins instead?"

She nods her head.

"Let's try to keep all the treats handheld. And display them on reusable trays," adds Kristen. "That way we're not being wasteful."

Stanley pouts a little. "I guess I'll bring more M&M cookies instead of limeade."

"Maybe you could bring limeade for us," I say. "We'll bring reusable cups."

Logan replies, "Good idea. I'll wash them, too!"

"It'll keep team spirits high," says Mariel, smiling.

Then Kristen shows us the blog with our pledge again, and we all approve.

As everyone works on banners and posters, I

come to a new realization. I am almost glad that saving the oceans is something I can't do alone. While I wish I could fix the oceans with a snap of my fingers, working with others and making new friends is pretty fun.

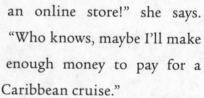

Chapter Twenty-Four

At last, it's the big day. As we prepare, Linda comes over with Biscuit. He is dressed in a Chihuahua-size shark costume to show team spirit. Linda proudly holds the five knitted bags she made for our bake sale.

"It's all I've worked on this week. I might start an online store!" she says. "Who knows, maybe I'll make enough money to pay for a Caribbean cruise."

I study all the different bags with their beautiful woven patterns.

"I love the aquamarine one."

"I'll make you one later," Linda says. "For free."

I give her a big hug and look up at her.

"Are you going to come to the bake sale?"

"Biscuit and I wouldn't miss it for the world," she replies.

Mom and Linda then compare their tote bags. Mom and I made five as well, but instead of yarn, ours are made out of zebra prints, polka dots, and canvas fabrics. Jenny soon comes over with her Vietnamese donuts. It's a quick stop because she needs to get ready for the recital.

To my surprise Vietnamese donuts don't look like regular donuts. They are more like balls of fried dough with sesame seeds on top. What they do share in common with regular donuts is they smell amazing, but as much as I want to try one, I don't touch them.

Nick pops his head out of his room.

"What's the big commotion?"

"We're getting ready for the bake sale," I reply. Biscuit barks in agreement.

"Sweet!" he says as he moves closer to investigate.

I show him all of our combined efforts, including the brownies I made with Mom. We made it with Mexican chocolate for an extra twist, which means they are a little spicy.

"Not bad, sis." Nick chews on a brownie. "They're pretty tasty."

I smile with my whole face.

"Are you coming to the bake sale?"

"Maybe. I have to work tonight, but we'll see." He looks a little sneaky like he might go, but I don't want to get my hopes up.

With a car jam-packed with goodies, we head to the dance studio. Stanley, Mariel, Logan, and Kristen meet us there early so we can set up our station.

We're greeted at the dance recital by Ms. Charlton, Jenny's dance teacher, who takes us to our selling spot. It's a prime location. We have three large folding tables near the main doors.

Ms. Charlton says, "I'm happy to have you guys here. I hope you sell a ton and raise a bunch of money."

After we're done setting up, our Sea Musketeer display looks amazing. On one table we have our different treats. On a separate table, we arrange the tote bags. On the third table we have the pledges and three-dimensional poster boards with all our oceans facts. Mariel brought her dad's laptop so people can look at the information on our blog and the fundraising page for the Marine Mammal Center. Then, strung above the tables, we have a large aquamarine banner that reads SAVE THE OCEANS!! in white lettering. Our spot looks practically perfect. Of course, we also have a great helper, Biscuit. He helps us simply by being adorable. People see him at the table and just naturally want to come over.

"How cute!" and "So adorable!" they all say.

As people trickle in to the recital, we attack them with our pledge signup sheets. Most people are happy to sign. Those who didn't said they would visit the blog later. The sale is going splendidly, and we almost run out of space on the pledge sheets before the performance starts.

We stop selling during the recital. The dancers range in age and so do the styles, but one thing is for certain: Jenny is definitely one of the best. Seeing her move beautifully on the stage makes me realize how much she loves it. I feel lucky to have a very talented best friend.

After the last dance, Ms. Charlton makes a few concluding remarks on stage. She begins by thanking all the dancers and parents, but then she mentions our group.

"Last but not least let's give a round of applause to the Sea Musketeers."

The audience gives us a standing ovation.

I turn *roja*, but this time it's a good thing. It's pride.

Suddenly I hear, "Look at my little sister."

I turn around and see Nick. He's wearing his pizza shop uniform and talking to Linda while putting down boxes of pizza. Biscuit is smitten with the scent of marinara sauce on his shirt.

"Nick!" I run over and hug him with both arms.

"I thought you weren't going to come," I say, looking up at him.

"I had to stop by. I needed to check it out as the official club mentor. I even brought some pizza. I convinced the pizzeria to donate some for you to sell and got a delivery driver to drop me off."

"That's amazing!" I exclaim. "The pizza will raise so much money."

I am filled with joy. While I know things are changing with my brother, I know he is there when I really need him.

At the end of the night, we count our earnings. We've raised almost a hundred dollars! We've also nearly sold out of our refreshments. There is just a little left for us all to nibble on. We need it, too, because we've been working hard all night.

"I'm so proud of you guys," says Linda, snacking on a Vietnamese donut.

"Here. Let me take a group picture." Mom motions at us with her phone to take a photo.

We gather in front of the display. I stand on the side, but everyone insists I stand in the middle with Biscuit.

"You're the club leader," says Stanley.

I stare at him.

"Am I?"

"Well, not officially," says Mariel, "but without you we wouldn't have done this. At least not together."

I pause. I've never considered myself a leader. I'm shy and quiet, but maybe leaders can be both.

"Quick vote. Who elects Stella leader of the group?" asks Jenny.

Everyone raises their hand.

"You're the leader, congrats," Logan says, smiling.

As Mom finally takes a picture, Kristen whispers, "We really should make T-shirts."

My mouth drops open in surprise. I hadn't thought of T-shirts.

"Okay, now smile," Mom says.

Flash. Mom takes a picture of me looking surprised . . . and happy. This night couldn't have gone any better.

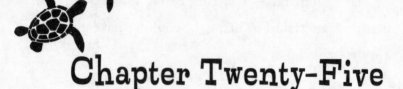

Chapter Twenty-Five

The next day, Mom donates all the money we earned from the bake sale to our fundraising page. I suddenly feel a little disappointed.

"It's not that much money, Mom. I wish it were millions."

"But, Stella, look—some people have donated to the page already."

I look at the total after she's posted our donation. It's nearly three hundred dollars. I guess our posters at the dance recital worked. Dad even donated twenty dollars.

"Plus, look at all the signatures you received on your pledge. That's more than a hundred people."

I eye all the names from our signup sheets. It's a lot.

"That's true," I reply.

"Changing this many people's behaviors is a big deal. Look at me—I mean, I carry around a tote bag everywhere now. That's all you."

I hug Mom. She's right. Because of me, she's one less person collecting plastic bags every day. The more people the Sea Musketeers reach, the more

plastic bags, straws, and bottles we will save from ending up in the ocean. That will make a *grande* difference.

The last days of summer are spent getting ready for school. I make sure to get a cool reusable drink container and new polka-dot shirts for school.

The group gathers one more time the weekend before school starts. This time we meet back at my house.

"Remember the game plan," I remind them. "First day of school, you've got to tell your class about the pledge."

"That will be easy for Jenny, Stella, and me," says Stanley. The three of us really lucked out this year being in the same classroom.

"Imagine if we can get everyone at our schools to sign the pledge. We'll be able to make a massive difference," says Logan.

We nod in agreement.

Mariel asks, "But what is the next event we're going to do? The Sea Musketeers can't stop now."

For a brief second, I feel a little anxious. I don't know what we'll do next. With some of us going to different schools, I'm afraid everyone will get too busy. I thought I'd never say it, but I don't want summer to end. I just feel like it's only really started. Especially now that I have new friends and a group of my own.

"Let's do another beach cleanup," says Logan.

"Oh, another bake sale!" Kristen exclaims.

"Or a dance marathon," replies Jenny.

Everyone starts shouting ideas, each a little wackier than the next. I sit back and relax. By the commotion of everyone in the room, I don't think I have anything to worry about.

Chapter Twenty-Six

On the first day of school, Mom takes us to a diner for breakfast. We have to go extra early in the morning because high school starts earlier than elementary school. It's one of those classic diners with old signs on the walls.

The three of us sit in a booth with red vinyl seats and order waffles. We can't make waffles at home, because we don't own a waffle maker. I look over at Nick. He's awfully quiet and pushing his waffle around his plate.

"Are you excited about high school?" I ask.

Nick shrugs.

"Kind of. It's strange to be starting a new school

again. I feel like I have to be more grown-up now. Plan for college, etc."

He looks wistfully at me.

"I sort of wish I could go back to elementary school with you."

"Me too." I lean on Nick.

"Well, you two can live with me forever," says Mom jokingly.

Nick rolls his eyes.

"And we can cancel the driving lessons," Mom says.

"No, no. I'm okay," he replies with a smirk.

"What about you, Stella? *¿Cómo te sientes?*"

It takes me a second. I feel so many things. Happy, excited, but then I settle on one word.

"I'm optimistic."

I really, really am.

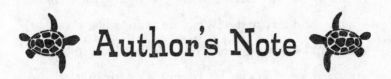 # Author's Note

Thank you for reading another adventure with Stella. Like the previous book, *Stella Díaz Has Something to Say*, there is so much of my own personal experiences in the book. I, too, have a Tía Maria in Oaxaca and love Chihuahuas. Like Nick, my older brother worked at a big chain pizzeria. It rhymes with Mominos.

But there are a few bigger differences now. Stella has grown into her own person and has become my voice for conservation—a subject I think many people are concerned with. I've also been inspired seeing how mobilized the younger generation has been on some tough topics. This motivated me to write this story and empower Stella.

While the book includes a few tips on reducing plastic, there is so much more you can do. I recommend doing your own brainstorming session with friends, family, and classmates. What are some other ways that you can be more green? And it doesn't have to be just plastic-related. It can be as simple as turning off the lights when you leave the room or walking or biking when you can, instead of driving. I also encourage you to look for things you can do in your own area. Maybe there is a community cleanup group where you can remove litter just like Stella does in the book. In fact, if you're in Chicago, you can go to one of the Shedd Aquarium's Great Lakes Action Days held a few times a year. Or use a tote bag! I never leave home without one!

More than anything, be thoughtful in the way you consume things. Try not to use something once and throw it away. Lastly, a kind reminder, don't beat yourself up. Being green can be overwhelming, and the news about pollution can be overwhelming. However, if we all cut back some and work together, it will make a big difference.

Finally, I wanted to share why I chose to use italics for the Spanish words in my books about Stella. This was a thoughtful decision for the sake of clarity and to make the story inclusive for all readers, especially ones who are Stella's age or younger who may not be familiar with Spanish or have trouble speaking it. I know firsthand how challenging it can be when you feel confused between the two languages. My hope is that all readers feel welcome to get to know Stella and join her adventures.

While there are many organizations and resources, here are a few I recommend if you would like to learn more about ocean conservation:

THE MARINE MAMMAL CENTER
marinemammalcenter.org

MISSION BLUE
mission-blue.org

NATIONAL GEOGRAPHIC KIDS
kids.nationalgeographic.com
/explore/nature/kids-vs-plastic

OCEANA
oceana.org

SAVE OUR SHORES
saveourshores.org

SHEDD AQUARIUM—GREAT LAKES ACTION DAYS
www.sheddaquarium.org
/Learning-Experiences/Teen-Programs
/Great-Lakes-Action-Days/

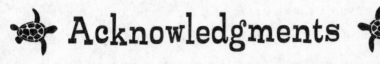 Acknowledgments

I'm delighted to be writing acknowledgments for the second time. First, I'd like to thank a few people I forgot to mention in the first book. Thank you to Nadia Husain, my former roommate, who gave me so much of the wonderful Chicago detail. I owe you a scoop from Oberweis. Thank you also to Mary Benedetto for your support and for reading so many of the early drafts of both books. I'd also like to thank many of the usual suspects like my mom; my boyfriend, Kyle; my brother, Alejandro; Mimi; Chris; Jessica; Elias; and Elanna. I love you all. Big shout-out to my friends Isabel, Amol, Kellie, Mariel, Eda, and Erika, too.

I'd also like to thank a few people involved in the

creation of this book. Thank you to my agent, Linda Pratt, and my great editorial team, Connie Hsu and Megan Abbate; there would be no book without you. A huge thank-you to Kristie Radwilowicz for her wonderful collaboration on the cover. Her charming, playful lettering makes me smile every time I see it. Thank you also to everyone at Roaring Brook Press including Jennifer Besser, Elizabeth Holden Clark, and Aimee Fleck. I have to also thank the marketing and publicity teams at Macmillan, especially Lucy Del Priore, Katie Halata, Melissa Croce, and Mary Van Akin. Thank you for championing this book and getting it into the hands of educators and librarians. You are rock stars!

Finally, I'd like to thank the people who have supported the first book and made the second book possible. These are the educators, the readers, SCBWI, and the bloggers. Knowing that you loved the first book gave me the confidence to write another *Stella*. For that, I'm truly grateful.

My family and me at the beach in Mexico.

Me at age 9

Questions for the Author

 Angela Dominguez

What did you want to be when you grew up?
I wanted to be a few different things, including a lawyer, director, and even an architect! However, what was a constant in my life was how much I loved to draw and my fascination with art. That ultimately led me to study art in college and eventually become an illustrator.

When did you realize you wanted to be a writer?
I've always loved reading books, and as a child I enjoyed making my own. Still, I was timid about sharing my stories. Even though we moved to the United States when I was very young, English is technically my second language. In school, I often made grammar errors, especially in my creative writing. At that time, I found it to be super embarrassing.

Thankfully, I had people in my life who told me I was a great storyteller, like my mom and my high school AP English teacher. That always stuck with me. Later, after a few years of illustrating, I realized that I wanted to tell stories to go with the characters I designed. With the encouragement of my literary agent, I decided to make the big leap. I am so glad that I did!

What's your most embarrassing childhood memory?

Yikes! They usually involve turning super *roja* (red). I do remember falling backward in my chair like Stella did in *Stella Díaz Has Something to Say*. That was awfully embarrassing.

What's your favorite childhood memory?

I have so many. It's hard to narrow it down, but I think my favorite memories usually surround being with my mom and brother. Our road trips and vacations were so much fun. We'd wake up super early, around three or four in the morning, to hit the road, and I'd stay up to keep my mom company. After sunrise, we'd stop by a diner for pancakes and a break. The open road was such an adventure.

What was your favorite thing about school?

School had its ups and downs for me. I was terribly shy like Stella, so presentations or meeting new kids was hard, but there was a lot that I did enjoy. I always loved learning, art class, and running in gym class. Math was especially fun in elementary school. History was awesome because it was like listening to an interesting story from the past. If I had to choose one thing, it was probably the library. The fact you are able to find a book on any subject and check it out is still amazing to me.

What were your hobbies as a kid? What are your hobbies now?

I loved to draw and read as a kid, so it's not much

different now. The big difference is that my hobbies are also part of my job description. While I'm really lucky that I get to do what I love, I've also had to find new hobbies to unwind, or I'd be thinking about work all the time. One of my favorite things to do now is to cook and bake. I'm obsessed with watching baking shows. I also love traveling and exploring the outdoors.

Did you play sports as a kid?
Not too much. I was usually nervous that I would make a mistake in front of everyone. Did I mention I was shy?

What book is on your nightstand now?
I still read children's books. They are wonderful! I'm currently reading *A Wish in the Dark* by Christina Soontornvat. I also recently finished *From the Desk of Zoe Washington* by Janae Marks, which I loved. Eventually, I'll circle back to a grown-up book. Maybe.

How did you celebrate publishing your first book?
I'm bad at celebrating my book birthdays. You spend so much time working on the book that when the actual book comes out it feels almost like a normal day. That said, I try to have a nice dinner with my boyfriend, and occasionally I'll have a small group of friends join us.

Where do you write your books?
I usually write in my office, but I will write on my couch with a knitted blanket when I want to feel cozy. I also

enjoy writing on the road, like on an airplane, on a train, or in a hotel room. Sometimes a change of location really helps your creativity or helps you see something from a new perspective.

What sparked your imagination for the Stella Díaz series?

It all started with a drawing of a girl with curly hair and a polka dot dress. Once I saw her, I knew I had to write a story for her. I eventually came up with this idea to do a picture book about a girl named Stella at an aquarium with her family. Her perfect day is ruined because there is a kid from school named Stanley who she is too shy to talk to. Instead of enjoying the exhibits, she keeps running away from him all day until she overcomes her fear.

While I still love that version, it didn't quite work as a picture book. People couldn't understand why Stella was so shy and couldn't speak to someone from school. Then I started thinking about why I was shy growing up and used my experiences as inspiration for the rest of the story. From there the story continued to grow and evolve. With some help from my amazing editor, it finally became a chapter book and now a series.

What is your favorite word?

That's tough! I love my family nickname, Teté. It means nothing in Spanish, but it feels like home when I hear it. I also love the word *jitomates*. It means "tomatoes" and it's used most commonly in Mexico. It's so fun to say! If I have to choose a word in English, it's probably *gregarious*. It means "friendly," and it sounds like it, too.

Who is your favorite fictional character?
I think I have to go all the way back to my childhood to choose my favorite, and it's Ramona Quimby, a character created by Beverly Cleary. I loved that she was opinionated and outspoken. While I might not have wanted to be exactly like her, I at least wanted her to be my best friend.

What was your favorite book when you were a kid? Do you have a favorite book now?
One of my all-time favorite books is *James and the Giant Peach* by Roald Dahl. My first-grade teacher, Ms. Bell, read it aloud to us, and I always looked forward to listening to her. The idea of visiting New York in a giant peach with large talking insects was magical and rather peculiar.

I love many books now, but I would say *Pie in the Sky* by Remy Lai and *Bob* by Rebecca Stead and Wendy Mass are pretty high up on my favorite kid books list.

If you could travel in time, where would you go and what would you do?
Sometimes I think it would be fun to visit the future. I'd like to see the new technology and hopefully see how we fixed some of our current problems. I would also like to ride around in a flying car. I was promised there would be flying cars, and I'd very much like to see one.

What's the best advice you have ever received about writing?

That writing, like most things in life, is not about getting it right on the first try. The first draft of your story is just to get ideas down onto paper. The revising is where the real magic happens. Same thing applies to drawing, too.

What advice do you wish someone had given you when you were younger?

If you struggle with shyness, you can work on it. There is nothing wrong with it, either, as long as it doesn't stop you from trying new experiences. Being reserved is also not a weakness. It just means you're introverted and like to observe. Those are wonderful qualities.

Do you ever get writer's block? What do you do to get back on track?

I definitely get writer's block. I usually take a walk or try reading a book. Reading is essential if you want to become a good writer. It helps show you what makes a good sentence and story.

What do you want readers to remember about your books?

That whether you're shy or come from a different place, everyone has something to say and it's worth hearing, too. I also hope they might laugh and relate to Stella and her adventures.

If you were a superhero, what would your superpower be?

I'd love to be able to teleport. Sometimes you really want to get somewhere very quickly, and sometimes you just want to hug your mom.

Do you have any strange or funny habits? Did you when you were a kid?

I like mustard with my scrambled eggs, which I think most people find weird. I also enjoyed eating anchovies as a toddler. Outside of food, as a kid I enjoyed hiding out underneath the living room table and drawing. I don't think that is very strange, but I did also draw on the actual table, too.

What do you consider to be your greatest accomplishment?

Truly, writing the Stella Díaz series. It was a dream to write a book like this and have it so well received. It really has been a delightful surprise.

What would your readers be most surprised to learn about you?

How often I talk to my dog, Petunia, during the day. She's just too cute!

Stella Díaz has big dreams—

but when the waters get rough, will she sink or swim? Find out in the third book of the award-winning Stella Díaz chapter book series.

Keep reading for an excerpt.

Chapter One

"Time for an adventure!" I exclaim.

"Stella? Where are you?" says Nick. I can hear his footsteps coming down the hall.

"I'm in here!" I shout.

"How can you even see in there?" Nick replies, calling to me through the door. "It's so dark."

I step out of the laundry closet wearing a headlamp. Nick quickly looks away from the blinding light.

He groans. "Whoa, what are you doing?"

"I'm getting ready to go camping in the

backyard with Jenny!" I flex my muscles. "It's going to be a real rough-and-tough adventure."

Nick clicks off my headlamp with his thumb and looks me in the eyes. "Stella, I'll believe it when I see it."

"Oh, you'll see," I reply, digging in my fanny pack.

Nick walks away. "Okay. Well, I'm going to be busy with my homework, so you two better stay out of trouble."

Nick has spent most of his Saturday at the kitchen table surrounded by a pile of books. Since Nick started ninth grade, his homework has more than doubled. Almost all his classes have a fat text-book, too. When I tried his backpack on once, I nearly fell backward from the weight of all the books. I want to be just like Nick when I'm in high school, but it's hard to imagine walking around with that backpack. Maybe when I'm his age, I can use two backpacks. That might help.

"You're just jealous you're not invited camping this time," I reply, putting my hands on my hips.

When we were younger, Nick and I would

occasionally camp out in the backyard. Because he's my big brother, he would take care of choosing the perfect spot for our tent and pitching it while I would draw in my sketchbook.

Nick snorts. "Sure. That's it, sis." Then he gets back to doing his homework.

According to my school's calendar, summer is over, but technically there are a few days left till it's autumn. Before we have to start wearing sweaters and parkas, my best friend, Jenny, and I want to make the most of the nice weather, which is why I suggested having a Saturday backyard sleepover. It's going to be so much fun. Sleepovers are already the best, but they're even better when they're outside.

When Jenny arrives, she hands me a glass casserole dish filled with spring rolls her mom made and says, "I have new dance moves to show you."

"Can't wait!" I reply, hugging the casserole. I can't wait for the spring rolls either.

With our arms full of camping equipment, we open the patio doors to go outside. We're hit with a refreshing breeze. It still feels like summer, but there is already an orange leaf or two on our oak tree hinting that fall is coming soon. The backyard is mostly quiet except for the rumble of the Metra, our local train line, in the distance.

I inhale deeply. "It's a perfect night for camping."

Jenny nods and looks at me. "Stella, have you ever been camping? My mom never wants to go. She thinks there will be too many bugs."

I turn *roja* like my red sleeping bag. I may look like an expert, but I've never been camping outside of my backyard in Chicago. Well, never *successfully*. Our family tried to go once in Wisconsin. Mom had seen pictures of a coworker's trip and thought it looked fun. We bought a ton of camping gear for this one trip, packed up our car, and drove out to the campsite. Then we unloaded everything, set up our tent . . . and realized how cold it was! We didn't last a whole night, even with a campfire nearby. We were asleep back in our beds before midnight. Ever since then, the camping gear mostly stays in our laundry closet except for adventures like tonight.

"No, but we're outdoors." I shrug my shoulders and add, "It's probably about the same."

Jenny looks at me wistfully. "I wish we were camping for real. Somewhere amazing, like Montana."

I nod. "But this is still fun! And I'm sure it's only a little bit different."

Jenny smiles and shakes her head as we get to work. She takes the poles out of the tent bag while I lay the tent flat on the ground. Then we snap each pole into place, making sure to get them all through the loops. Like magic, our tent pops up.

"Can I show you some of my new choreography now?" Jenny asks eagerly.

Recently, Jenny joined a new dance class. It meets once a week, but she proudly tells me that it's much harder than her dance summer camp. She's even dancing with the older girls, too!

She stands on our small backyard deck, her makeshift stage, and I sit down on the grass below.

Just as Jenny begins to twirl on her tippy-toes, I spy a shadowy figure peeking out from the patio door.

Nick yells, "Yeah, this is real rugged camping!"

I stick my tongue out at him.

He snickers. "I'll leave you two alone with the elements. Give me a shout when you get hungry."

Then he closes the door.

Jenny ignores him and continues with her performance. For the grand finale, she even leaps! I clap when she bows at the end.

"Brava!" I cheer.

Next we put the finishing touches on our campsite. Once we make our tent cozy with lanterns, pillows, and our spring roll rations, we jump inside and zip the door shut.

"What now? Should we draw?" I ask, scratching my head. I'm not quite sure what people do when they go camping. I start searching my fanny pack for pencils.

Jenny replies, "Well, we could tell ghost stories."

I grab a pillow. "I don't know, Jenny. I don't like scary stories." My shoulders tense up just thinking about it.

"Let's try one. Scary stories are part of the sleepover experience," she says knowingly.

As Jenny begins to tell a story about a dark and stormy night, the wind suddenly picks up. The leaves start to rustle, and the branches creak on the oak tree. The noises from the Metra now sound like ghostly whistles. I quickly realize that we're absolutely alone in the backyard, with only a nylon tent to protect us.

Jenny pauses and turns toward me. She looks nervous. "Did you hear that?"

"What? Did you hear something?" I squeeze my pillow even tighter. I didn't hear anything, but maybe Jenny has super hearing.

We look at each other. Suddenly we hear what sounds like a branch cracking above our heads. Without saying a word, we jump out of the tent and run back inside the house.

As we close the patio door behind us, I turn to Jenny.

"Good thing we're not in Montana."

She nods and locks the door.

Chapter Two

While we are pretty sure there is nothing in the backyard, Jenny and I end up sleeping in the living room, just in case. Nick helps me put *The Undersea World of Jacques Cousteau* on the television so that Jenny and I can fall asleep to Jacques's gentle French accent.

Watching Jacques and his group exploring the oceans is captivating. The whooshing sound of the divers breathing heavily in their scuba masks also makes my eyes heavy.

"I almost forgot!" Jenny says, sitting up in her sleeping bag.

"What?" I ask, yawning. All the commotion must have made me sleepy.

"You're going to love this."

I roll over. "Tell me in the morning."

"My mom registered me for swimming classes at the YMCA."

I pop up. "You're right. I want to join!"

On the first day of fourth grade, I made a list of dreams for the school year. Big dreams, like win an award, work on a big project, and make new types of art, just to name a few. I even wrote *Nobel Prize*, but I had to cross it out. Turns out they don't have one just for kids. While swim lessons might not be on my official list, swimming does sound fun. I guess I'll just have to add it to the list.

"Yes! I bet my mom could drive you, too. It's only on Wednesdays, and the session starts in two weeks," Jenny says.

I nod. "I'll ask my mom when she gets home."

I look at the clock on

the TV stand. It's almost 10:00 P.M., and Mom's still not home yet. She is at her first-ever "Girls' Night" with her coworkers at the radio station. Now that Nick is fifteen and can officially babysit me alone, Mom is beginning to hang out with work friends a bit more. I'm happy for her, but it's awfully late, and I want to ask her about the swim lessons right now. Plus, I can't really fall asleep until Mom tucks me in and says, "*Te quiero, mi estrellita.*"

To which I always reply, "I love you, too, Mom."

I try to stay awake so I can see her when she gets home, but Jacques Cousteau's voice is too soothing. I fall fast asleep and dream of swimming in the deep blue sea.

In the morning, I wake up to the smell of batter and the sound of Mom humming. Jenny and I head to the kitchen to investigate.

"*Buenos días.* How did the sleepover go, *niñas?*" Mom says, flipping a pancake over. "I noticed that you two decided not to sleep outside."

We start giggling just thinking about our

adventure last night. The only way I can sum it up is to say, "Camping was an experience."

"*Muy interesante*." She laughs. "You'll have to tell me more about it later."

Mom hands us plates, and we serve ourselves breakfast. Jenny devours her pancakes with lakes of maple syrup on top.

"I never get to eat this at home," Jenny says in between bites. "Our pancakes are way different."

She pours more maple syrup onto her plate.

Jenny's mom makes pancakes, but they are Vietnamese-style. Their pancakes are made out of rice flour and filled with meat or veggies. I've had them at her house, and they're yummy, but they are definitely not syrupy sweet like this.

When Jenny's mom arrives to pick her up, Jenny whispers to me at the front door, "Don't forget to ask your mom about swim lessons."

"I'm on it," I reply, giving her a high five.

I help Mom clean up in the kitchen. She leaves out one plate of pancakes, ready for when Nick finally wakes up. She even put chocolate chips in his batch because those are his favorites.

"How was Girls' Night?" I ask. Then I lean in closer and make my voice stern. "And when exactly did you get home, young lady?"

"*Perdonéme, jefa*," she teases, calling me her boss. "Ten forty-two in the evening. I gave you a kiss on the cheek, but you were wiped out."

"Oh," I reply. That's not so late. Camping must have really made me tired!

She continues, "And Girls' Night was so much fun! I haven't been salsa dancing like that in a long time!"

She busts out into a salsa move in the middle of the kitchen. It's like her feet and hips are twisting with joy.

I frown. Mom and I salsa together all the time. Every Friday we have what she likes to call our "weekly appointment." That's our Friday night tradition where Nick, Mom, and I play games and have family fun time. And Mom and I always end up salsa dancing all around the living room.

Mom sees my face and knows I'm upset.

"*Mi amor*, I misspoke. I know that you and I salsa, but it's different with a live band. *El ritmo* just takes over."

The rhythm must be taking her over now, too, because she cha-chas again.

I nod. I sort of understand. I also know that when we're salsa dancing, Mom slows down for me. I remember when Mom and Dad used to salsa together. Her feet would move at triple the speed. I could never understand how she did it. Suddenly this conversation gives me an idea.